The Heirloom

A NOVEL

The Heirloom

A NOVEL

Joe Blakely

CraneDance Communications Publishers
a wing of BGleason Design & Illustration, LLC
Eugene, Oregon

CraneDance Communications Publishers,
PO Box 50535, Eugene, Oregon 97405
©2004 Joe Blakely   All Rights Reserved
First Edition, 2005

Library of Congress Cataloging-in-Publication Data
Blakely, Joe

A novel set in Bandon, Oregon, in the 1920s about the historic
Nestlé condensed milk factory, loggers and moonshiners, the
Coast Guard and a wild sea adventure around Cape Horn.

Cover images from the collection of the Bandon
Historical Society Museum in Bandon, Oregon.

ISBN 0-9708895-3-4

Dedication

I wish to dedicate this book to Louis D. Felsheim. Mr. Felsheim bought the Bandon *Western World* newspaper in 1913 and was its publisher and editor through the 1920s. It is through his journalistic excellence that I was provided a glimpse back in time. Louis Felsheim was a courageous editor on this country's rugged western frontier, and I have the greatest admiration for this man.

Please remember, however, that this is a book of fiction and the editorials I put forth are not his writing: they are mine.

In addition I would like to dedicate this book to Saundra L. Miles, my financée.

Author's Note

This novel was inspired by an old 1920 photograph I found in the Bandon Historical Society Museum. It was this photograph that led me to write a short history of the Nestlé building (which was later published in the *Oregon Historical Quarterly*). At the time of writing that article, I was seized with the idea of writing a novel with Bandon as the stage.

Many factors supported the fact that it could be a fascinating story. There was the huge Nestlé's Food Company, (the largest in the United States) and its battle with the union known as the Dairyman's League; there was the United States Coast Guard which had grown out of the Life Saving Service of 1915; there was the burgeoning lumber industry and the illegal trade of moonshine; and of course there was the ever-present danger of sea, storms, and ship wrecks. And at the time, a few windjammers still sailed around Cape Horn. Needless to say I was intrigued to the point of writing this novel.

Acknowledgements

I would like to thank a number of people for helping me with this book. This novel has been a dream of mine for the last five years. My dream was set in motion when I contacted Barbara Gleason, of BGleason Design and CraneDance Communications Press, who started putting my novel into the framework of a book. It is her genius that created the cover.

I had help from a number of editors including the main editor, Dorene Ferguson, who gave my story cohesion and depth, my brother Larry Blakely, my fiancée, Saundra Miles, and of course, Barbara Gleason, the final examiner. Other people I would like to thank are Judy Knox, curator of the Bandon Historical Society Museum who was helpful in giving me access to materials in their archives and in finding the pictures that grace this book's cover. Dow Beckham's book, *Bandon by the Sea,* was very helpful, and a special thanks goes to Dow for an interview he gave me, when he told me what riding on a stern-wheeler was like in the 1920s. The Bandon *Western World* newspaper was an invaluable source in understanding the times. Of course, there were many other people who gave me help and I thank all of them. They helped make my dream a reality.

Blakely The Heirloom

Chapter 1
John's Decision

John Dowd let fly a two handed set shot from half court and it swished through the net, completing a perfect arc. The Franklin High School junior barely heard the ecstatic cheers of his teammates and the explosion from the bleachers. This was a scrimmage game and John's team had just won. Coach Edmiston loved this guy John Dowd. He pounded the shoulders of his assistant and yelled, "This kid is the best I've ever coached, the best I've ever even seen!"

The cheers were still ringing in the gym when Coach Edmiston noticed the double doors at the far end of the gym open, admitting an officer from the Portland Police Department, who came over to the team bench. There was something in the officer's face that made Coach Edmiston catch his breath. He heard the words cupped into his ear, nodded, and waved John over to the bench. "John, let's go to my office."

"John, Officer Wren has some very bad news."

Wren, grim faced, pulled up a chair close to where John was sitting. His badge was gleaming in the poorly lit room. "John, a terrible tragedy has happened. This afternoon your mother and father were on a drive along the Columbia Gorge. Your father lost control of their Model T and it went over a cliff. John, I'm sorry, your father and mother were killed instantly. I want you to know your father was the best police officer on the Portland Police Force. It is a tragic loss to us as well as to you."

John was dumbfounded and he sat, stunned. But when the words finally registered, he began to cry and tears flooded down his cheeks. Both the coach and officer put their arms around John in an effort to console him.

Coach Edmiston drove John home. They sat outside in the dark car, and the rain splattered on the windshield. Edmiston didn't know what to say, and John couldn't say anything. Later that evening, Officer Wren and two other policemen gave John the few personal items found in the wrecked car. His mother's gloves and purse, her wedding ring, and the watch. The Hamilton watch his father always carried, always checked the time by flipping it open, the click as it shut. John stared at the gold watch, felt its weight in the palm of his hand, and remembered his father's voice.

"John," his father had said, "someday I will give this valuable watch to you, and you must treasure it." He flipped the lid open. "Notice this inscription on the inside lid. 'In the confusion of life persevere.' The watch was given to me by my mother when I reached my eighteenth birthday. It had been your grandfather's finest possession."

John now felt that this watch was his finest possession; plus it was his only connection to his deceased parents whom he would miss dearly. He showed the watch to each officer, opened it and showed them the inscription. He gently closed the lid and felt the cool metal in his hands, then he quickly latched the chain snap to his trouser belt loop and stuck the watch in his pocket. He'd seen his father do just this motion, how many times? He could feel its coolness against his thigh through the fabric of his trouser pocket. He thanked the officers again and again for bringing him this precious item. This watch would give him courage to face the unknown. With the tears finally abating, he showed the police to the door. Once they were gone, he whispered out loud, "What will I do now?"

The next morning John felt very much alone. Toast and coffee were a comforting routine. He started reading the morning's *Oregonian*, June 12, 1921. John was his parent's only child. At just eighteen, he imagined that being on his own meant he might not be able to finish his senior year. He knew his strength was in his athletic ability. Every coach he'd ever had drilled it into him, he was a natural. He could run, he could snatch any kind of ball out of the air, he drove himself and his team beyond every boundary.

He lamented the fact that he hadn't done better in his academic classes. In one class he remembered his teacher saying, "Those students who haven't read their assignment this morning might as well leave the class room. There is no room in here for slackers. John, did you read the pages I assigned to the class?"

"No sir."

"This is the third time John! I won't stand for this," the instructor said. "Leave my classroom at once!"

As John left the classroom that day, he heard the other students laughing at him. That embarrassment had hurt him deeply. He remembered similar embarrassment in his math class, too. Maybe he wouldn't mind leaving these classroom experiences behind. Leaving the hurt was all right. He'd miss the attention he got from the girls, though. Just last week

Arline Robinson had waited after the Friday night game. He'd spotted her in the stands, and there she was, waiting. She'd told him he was handsome, that she loved his dark hair and his even darker eyes. And his smile. He'd never forget how she said that, either.

Taking a large sip of the hot coffee John scalded his tongue and lip. As the descending coffee funneled its burning way down his throat, John thought about his options. Should he take a part time job that would allow him to complete his senior year of high school, or should he find a full time job? If he could find a part time job he would still be able to play sports and complete his schooling. It appeared that this was the right decision to make. He thought of coming home to this house every evening, of eating his dinner alone, of going to bed each night without the sound of his mother's, "'night, my darling son," and his father's snores from the end of the hall. The thought of working full time, leaving Portland and this tragedy behind began to look more attractive.

As he read the paper he noticed an advertisement for a job opportunity.

> "Needed: A man to load and unload ships in Bandon, Oregon. The job is being offered by the Nestlé condensed milk factory. A Nestlé representative will be conducting interviews and taking applications at the train station today."

John went to see the Nestlé representative at the Southern Pacific train depot. There were only a few people lined up in front of a small office that was right next to the clerks selling tickets. John waited patiently as the people in front of him went into the office and left. At last it was his turn. The representative gruffly stated to him, "You're pretty young to be looking for work so far from home. Bandon's a remote town on the south coast of Oregon."

John explained to the man his current dilemma and why he was seeking work.

"I was really looking for someone with a good work record, someone strong that would learn quickly the responsibilities of a new job. I would like to find someone who had work experience in a condensary."

John felt for the watch in his pocket. He didn't know what a condensary was. "I am strong, and feel that I could learn this job, if you'll give me a chance."

John could feel the man's glaring eyes looking him over, appraising him. After a long hesitation the man said, "I think I will take a chance on you. Could you be ready to leave day after tomorrow?"

"Yes sir, yes sir! And thank you, sir," John said, standing and offering his right hand.

"Before you leave let's go to the ticket window and I'll buy you a train ticket that will take you to Coquille. From Coquille you will take the Nestlé stern-wheeler to Bandon." After purchasing the ticket the man said, "Good luck, young man."

The next day John was very busy. First he attended the burial of his parents. Because his father had been a Portland police officer, many officers attended and praised his father's service to Portland's citizens. John found tears in his eyes more than once, and he laughed loudly to hear of some of the stories about his father. Could he ever hope to live up to the high standards set by his father?

After the ceremony he rushed home and began packing his suit case in readiness for his trip south the next morning. He could hardly believe it. He was leaving Portland behind and embarking on a strange new journey. His family heirloom watch would give him the courage to confront the uncertain future.

Blakely The Heirloom

Chapter 2

John Arrives in Bandon

Bandon was a pleasant thought in John's mind, an escape from his recent tragedy. As the train steamed along the banks of the Coquille River, John pulled out his pocket watch and noted the time: 3:15 p.m. He put the watch back in his pocket and remembered what the Nestlé representative had instructed: once in Coquille, he had but thirty minutes to board the stern-wheeler. As the train approached Coquille, John heard the loud steam-generated whistles explode, echoing throughout the valley, pastures and mountains. It was a pleasant crescendo reminding people that the train ran on schedule. The train slowed and came to a stop on the outskirts of Coquille at precisely 3:30 p.m.

John got off the train, looked up the dirt street and saw the large two-story Richmond-Barker Building, with its prominent sign, "Farmers and Merchants Bank." He saw people standing in small groups outside the bank on the wood boardwalks. He noticed the main dirt street heading into town was filled with people, horse drawn wagons, and even a few cars. It was a mild 80 degrees on that Wednesday in the middle of June. Reaching into his pocket he pulled out his watch: 3:40 p.m. He had twenty minutes to catch the stern-wheeler.

He walked towards the front of the train looking for the stern-wheeler. Steam was pulsating out from the engine. He stopped a porter to ask for directions, and he pointed to the large warehouse at the river's edge: "Nestlé Condensary Warehouse." Tied up on the river side of the warehouse was the huge stern-wheeler, the *John Wilde*. John saw the beautiful boat, its steam stack jutting fifteen to twenty feet in the air. He could see passengers strolling around the walkway on the second level. On the lower level he could see the cargo being loaded and animals herded in, and at the rear of the boat he saw the huge steam-operated paddle wheel.

Passengers, cargo, milk cans, and animals vied for entry. Finally, John made it on board and, with his suitcase in hand, climbed the stairs to the second level. Before he could find a place to sit, the large paddle began to churn as steam belched from the stack. John checked his watch and noted that the stern-wheeler had pushed away from the dock at exactly 4:00 p.m. John dropped his suitcase on a seat in the passenger compartment and raced outside to a rail position to watch as the town of Coquille and the Nestlé's Warehouse receded from view. John's excitement heightened as the large craft moved slowly west towards the ocean, the town of Bandon, and his new job at the Nestlé's Food Company.

As the stern-wheeler made its way to Bandon, it made frequent stops at dairymen's docks all along its route. A passenger told John that the ship would stop about one hundred times, "It's a long slow trip." As the ship approached each dock, John could see the ten-gallon milk cans lined up and waiting. The boat's crew would remove the filled cans from the dock and replace them with empty cans, and this was all done as the ship slowly cruised past. Sometimes John would see passengers waiting with the milk cans, and they would hop onto the stern-wheeler during this loading and unloading process.

About eight miles away from Bandon, John was still at the rail, watching. At another dock, he read the big hand-carved sign: "Adam and Jane Bennett's Dairy." He saw the Bennett farm house, two stories with a gabled roof that was pierced in the center by a chimney. The house was raised up off the ground several feet in case of high water. From the front porch a gangway extended out to the river dock. John couldn't help but notice that along with the milk cans on the Bennett dock, there was also a young lady, a beautiful young lady.

John watched as the young woman boarded the ship. On the run she hurled her small stature across the gap between dock and boat. John waited several minutes, giving the girl enough time to enter, climb the stairs and find a seat on the passenger deck. John finally left his rail vantage point and ambled inside, trying to look causal. The girl was sitting right next to his suitcase. She was lovely. Beautiful wavy brown hair, a lower lip much larger than the top as if she were in a constant pout, and of slight build with a substantial bosom. Her big blue eyes sparkled as she smiled at John and the pout turned into a gorgeous smile. Overwhelmed, John sat down on the other side of his suitcase, and as he did so he noticed out of the corner of his eye that she was looking at him. Just then the boat hit some sort of river obstruction (sand or a large log) and both instinctively tried to catch John's suitcase as it bounced off the seat.

John looked at her in surprise and said, "There is nothing in it that will break, but thank you for helping me catch it."

"You're welcome," the girl said. "My name is Mary, what's yours?"

John blurted out his name, and said, "I'm on my way to Bandon and a new job at the Nestlé's Food Company. Do you know anything about that business?"

Relaxing back in her seat, Mary told John about the plant. "The reason I know so much about the plant is because I did a report on it for my English class. My family has been supplying milk to the canned milk factory for about a year now. It is the largest condensary in the United States. They have over a hundred employees. They make condensed whole milk and condensed sweet milk. They have huge markets for the milk in the Orient. Since their arrival in Bandon, the dairy industry has boomed. You probably noticed all the dairies along the Coquille River. Nestlé buys milk from all of them. Plus, there is a huge dairy industry blossoming to the south of Bandon. What job have they hired you to do?"

The more Mary talked the more infatuated John became with her. She was so open, so alive, and when she smiled John almost fell off his seat. He felt tongue tied as he responded to her question but she didn't seem to notice at all.

Recovering slightly, John said, "I've been hired to load and unload ships at Nestlé." He went on to explain to Mary about his parents' untimely death, and his imminent need to support himself. He told her of his decision to leave the life he had known, this travel south and this new adventure. Looking into Mary's concerned eyes, he now knew he had made the right decision. He told Mary of his high school exploits, that he had been a star athlete, and that he had expected to lead his school's team to state championships had he been able to finish his senior year. Mary's eyes grew big as if accepting what John said as truth. "But this is the most important thing I have now," he said, pulling the watch from his pocket. "My heirloom watch," he carefully handed it to Mary.

Mary opened the watch and read the inscription, "In the confusion of life persevere." Then she whispered, "I wonder what the hidden meaning of these words are?" She gently snapped the cover closed, turned it over in her hand and said, "Hamilton." Then she gave it back to John.

John was aware that as passengers walked by and mingled in the enclosed area some would nod to Mary. Looking out the windows, John could see the pasture lands and behind them mountains covered with tall trees as the stern-wheeler slowly made its way down the river. After a while, John lost track of what was going on inside and outside the boat as he became more involved in his conversation with Mary, and he grew comfortable in her presence.

"I have lived in Bandon my whole life, and this will be my senior year at Bandon High School. My fiancé graduated this year. He's leaving for college on the East coast tomorrow. When he returns, in about four years, we plan to marry. The reason I am going into town today is to spend our last day together before he leaves."

John clutched the watch: a fiancé? It's not what he wanted to hear but he did not let her know. He was crestfallen. She was the loveliest creature he'd ever met and he wanted to see her again. His thoughts traveled many times faster than the steamboat. Bandon was too close, this meeting must go on forever, he said in his heart.

In the next few minutes both Mary and John were buffeted about as the boat eased into its berth at the Bandon dock. John raced to the window and watched as the crew tied the big boat to the dock. Grabbing his suitcase he led Mary down the stairs and then, still holding her hand in his, he helped her jump from the boat to the dock. Once on the dock, John looked into Mary's eyes. Her eyes were riveted on his.

"It was nice meeting you," Mary said.

"It was nice meeting you, too. I would like to see you again."

"I come into town once a week to buy groceries for my parents, maybe then," Mary said. A young man rushed onto the dock. "Mary! I've been waiting for you. We must get going. I have so much to tell you." He turned to John, and said, "Who is this?" John reluctantly let go of Mary's hand and found himself face to face with Mary's fiancé.

"John, I would like you to meet Earl Jacob, my fiancé. Earl, this is John Dowd." The two men shook hands. John's clench tested the strength of Earl's grasp. John felt his insides boil over with jealousy. His hand returned to his watch pocket, the cool gold soothing the hurt. But there was still tension as Earl looked at him.

"We have to get going, I haven't much time." Earl nodded in John's direction and led Mary off in the direction of town.

Chapter 3
Earl's Decision

Earl Jacob, the son of Tom Jacob, president of the First National Bank of Bandon, had just graduated from high school and was preparing to go away to college. Earl was five feet six inches tall, with a slender build, dark red hair, piercing blue eyes, and freckles. He had been chosen president of his high school class, and had participated in all high school team sports and had excelled in academics, so much so, that he had been offered a scholarship to Harvard College.

Earl knew his parents, Tom and Betty Jacob, beamed with pride knowing he had been admitted to the prestigious Harvard. Only one obstacle remained in the path of this grand opportunity, and that obstacle was Mary Bennett. They had done everything together: walked among the giant cedars, firs and spruces, fished, hunted, danced, studied, played, and kissed. Earl loved Mary with all his heart; yet he knew he had to experience life away from Bandon. He looked forward to college and living away from home, but the thought of leaving his beautiful Mary behind was almost too much for Earl. He wanted to take Mary with him but also knew that Mary had to stay in Bandon to help her parents with their small dairy.

The sun was directly above them as they walked along the shoreline; it was a warm eighty degrees, and beautiful white clouds adorned the blue sky. The warm day was cooled by the ocean spray that flew off the white crested waves as they lazily rolled in for as far as the eye could see. Earl felt refreshed walking next to the water. They found the deer trail that led through a Sitka spruce forest and up the cliffs to their remote hideaway; they had shared this secret spot for many years, discovering it as children. The vista seemed endless and breathtakingly beautiful. Far below them Earl heard the waves as they crashed against gigantic rocks and watched as the ocean spray rose and evaporated in the warm air. Seagulls darted up from the cliff's edge, rising high above them.

Mary spread out the blanket on the ground. Earl slowly descended into her arms and they embraced and kissed for a long time.

Finally, Mary broke the enraptured moment and blurted out, "Earl I don't want you to leave. I just don't know what I will do without you here." She began to cry.

"Mary, we've been over this so many times. I must go. My parents say I can't afford to miss this opportunity for the best education in the world."

Staring off towards the ocean Mary said, "But what do *you* believe? Is it just your parents you listen to?" Earl had no answers, at least not ones she would listen to. He stood up, stretched, ran his fingers through his hair and looked down at Mary, "You know I don't want to leave you. But, you will be fine without me, we'll write a lot, and when I return it will be as though I had never left. My parents love you, too." It was hard for Earl to keep from crying. Earl lowered himself and once more they enjoyed the intimacy of their love. They stayed in each others arms for the rest of the afternoon kissing and talking, each hoping the day would never end.

As the sun eased toward the horizon, they reluctantly pulled themselves apart, picked up their belongings and began their journey back to Bandon. Earl knew he had to start preparing for his trip east and he knew Mary had to return to her milking duties on her parent's farm. When they reached town, they had one last passionate embrace. Earl touched the tears that were streaming down Mary's face; Mary turned her face away. Earl kissed her on the neck. "Goodbye," he whispered, and somberly trudged off towards his home. He turned back one time and saw Mary. The blanket filled her arms, and her head was down. She ran towards the Bandon docks.

Blakely

The Heirloom

Chapter 4
Mrs. Smith's Boarding House

With Mary and Earl gone, John was confronted with the problem of where he was going to spend the rest of the day and night. Dejected by Mary's sudden departure, he looked around at his new surroundings. Bandon's bay was filled with ships resting on the still water: a four-masted windjammer, three schooners all loaded down with logs, one steamer, many small fishing boats, and one Coast Guard launch. And on each of the vessels, John saw workers loading and unloading cargo.

"Are you John Dowd?" John turned toward the gruff voice. Before him was a young man with wild eyebrows that flared up as though waiting for John to answer his question.

"Yes sir, I am John Dowd."

"I'm Robert Crowe, Assistant Supervisor for the Nestlé's Food Company," he said, shaking John's hand. "I'm here to show you to your quarters." Crowe bent down and picked up John's suitcase, and as he stood, he adjusted the light-rimmed glasses back up on the bridge of his nose and smiled. John noticed Crowe's slim build and dark brown hair that was parted down the middle. "I have arranged a room for you to rent. I think you will like what I've found. You'll be staying at Mrs. Nora Smith's boarding house. She has room for four boarders. She lost one guy recently so you will be filling that vacancy. The cost of the room includes meals and she'll wash your clothes once a week. Her husband died in a logging accident and she needs the money from her rentals to help pay for her living expenses. Let's get going."

As they walked, John told Robert of his decision to take the Nestlé job and his love of sports, basketball most of all. "You're an athlete? That's fine because I think of myself as one, too. In fact I'm considering starting a basketball team in October that will represent our plant. Would you be interested in playing on a basketball team?"

Not believing his ears, John responded without hesitation. "Yes, sir!" After a few more steps, John asked, " How long have you worked for Nestlé?"

"About two years now. They hired me just after I graduated from Oregon Agricultural College over in the valley, at Corvallis. I started out in the shipping and receiving department, and since then I have moved to management with jobs that have more responsibility. We are the biggest condensed milk factory on the Pacific Coast."

Robert pointed at the house ahead of them. "That's Mrs. Smith's Boarding house on the corner."

It was a white, two story structure with blue shuttered windows that looked down on the town of Bandon. The front yard was contained by a picket fence and a riot of summer flowers. As they walked through the open gate and up the porch steps, John could see Mrs. Smith waiting behind the screen door. She opened the squeaky door and invited them in. They stepped inside, and she let the screen close behind them.

"I would like you to meet John Dowd, Nora. He's Nestlé's new employee that I told you about."

Mrs. Smith wiped her plump hand on her flowered

apron and offered it to John. He took her hand in his own. Mrs. Smith said, "This is fortunate because you have arrived right at dinner time. Julia!" She called to her daughter, "Show John his room."

"John, as soon as you have washed up, come down for dinner." John didn't need Mrs. Smith to tell him dinner was nearly ready, the aromatic smells made it obvious.

With the greetings over, Robert dismissed himself saying, "John, we'll expect to see you tomorrow morning at 8 a.m. Report to my office first so I can show you around the plant." Robert pushed the screen door open and left.

On the way up the stairs, John saw the dining room off to his left. The dining table was huge, and there were already three young men seated, waiting for dinner to be served. Three more chairs were empty, and John's stomach rumbled in anticipation of the coming meal.

"John, your room is the first one on the right," said Julia. Once up the stairs, John saw a hallway with two doors on either side, and he opened the first one on his right: his new home. Julia whispered, "Just a word of warning for you to be careful, because one of our boarders is a logger with a mean disposition. I'm hoping he will leave our house soon and find some place else. My mother feels the same way, too. Hurry, we are about to dish up dinner."

John emptied the contents of his suitcase, hung his few shirts and trousers in what passed for a closet curtained into one corner of the room, and the rest went in one of two drawers in an oak dresser. He glanced out the window. He had a beautiful view of Bandon's bay and could see the Nestlé plant plus the ships. Smoke shot into the evening sky from Nestlé's towering smoke stacks. He washed his hands in a bowl of water that was on a table before rushing back down the stairs.

Spread out on the large dining room table was a large bowl of mashed potatoes, a platter of meat covered with rich brown gravy, green beans, and fresh baked rolls. There were pitchers of milk and lemonade, and a steaming pot of coffee. John guessed that the other diners were about his age, maybe a little older. He took the chair on the stair-side of the table, and Nora Smith took the seat at the head of the table. Julia sat down last, once she had made sure everything was on the table.

Mrs. Smith introduced John to the men and then said, "Enjoy your dinner. You can all get acquainted later."

There wasn't much conversation, just the polite, "Please pass the potatoes," and the sounds of silverware. John noticed the big man across from him, probably the logger Julia had mentioned, had a prominent furrow in his forehead right between his eyes, eyes that glared at John throughout the entire meal. After dinner John retired to his room. He looked out the window at the lights shining on the water in the bay. While he couldn't quite shake the sensation that there was something evil in the house, he still felt happy about the way things were working out. He undressed, making sure that his watch stayed safely tucked in his trouser pocket. He lay down on his back in the strange bed and, for a while, stared at the ceiling. His last thought, before he sank into a deep sleep, was about Mary Bennett.

Chapter 5

Just one of the boarders, Jake, was at breakfast when John bounded down the stairway. As John sat down at the table, he saw Julia entering the dining room from the kitchen, carrying fresh oatmeal and toast. She put the food in front of John.

"Would you like some coffee?"

"Yes." As the word slipped from John's lips his cup was filled with the hot steamy liquid. John looked around the room. He saw a cupboard filled with old dishes, wallpapered walls, and a swinging door that separated the dining room from the kitchen.

John couldn't help noticing how much like her mother Julia was. She was energetic and becomingly plump, yet with a youthful bounce and beauty all her own. Her golden hair was drawn up in a bun on both sides of her head with a straight part down the middle. She had a constant smile and rosy cheeks in a pleasant oval face. John remembered Jake from the introductions last night, and John sensed that Jake seemed a little jealous at all the attention John was receiving from Julia.

"Where are you from, John?" Jake asked.

John told him his memorized reply: from Portland, parents died in an accident, job at Nestlé was his means of support. He ventured some more about the stern-wheeler from Coquille, and actually told Jake about meeting Mary Bennett, thinking that Jake might not be so jealous of Julia if he knew John was interested in another local girl. "Jake, where are you from?"

"I was raised in Port Orford," Jake responded. "My father works for the U.S. Coast Guard, formerly known as the Life Saving Service. He has a medal for heroism. My mother is a school teacher. When I turned eighteen, my father told me I had to leave home to find my own future. That's when I came here and began work for the Nestlé's Food Company."

While pouring coffee for Jake, Julia said, "Jake, I didn't know your father worked for the Coast Guard. That is so exciting. You must be very proud of him, getting a medal for his bravery." John saw a warmth in Julia's face as she poured Jake's coffee. While refilling John's cup she said, "You are lucky you didn't have to eat with Luther and Matt. They always make my day start out so glum. Luther talks of all the fights he gets into, how he beats people up if they get out of line or challenge his position. He makes himself seem so righteous and those he beats up as insignificant. And Matt, he's the little guy. He hangs around with Luther just because Luther's so big and mean. The two of them work at the same logging company. I feel like an anvil has been lifted off my chest when they leave. You two make my day brighter!" As Julia cleared the dining table while John and Jake finished eating, she said, "Sometimes I wish I worked in the plant. I could walk with you to work and make some money for myself."

Jake said, "We have twenty-five women working there now. I can tell Mr. Crowe that you want a job if you would like me to."

"Oh, you probably shouldn't. My mother really needs me here. She sometimes drinks a little too much, and if I were to leave her all alone during the day, there's no telling what would happen. She needs my help and companionship for now. But maybe later on.

Wait here, I'll get your sack lunches."

Jake, lunch sack in hand, pushed his one hundred and fifty pounds against the screen door. It squeaked open with ease. His five foot eight inch frame passed through the threshold and outside into a cloudless cool morning. John followed behind Jake, laughing to himself as he noticed Jake's ears from behind. They stuck out, noticeably so, on each side of his head, a head that was covered with blond hair. Jake's face was rectangular and his nose and chin were pointed. As they hurried off to work, they could hear the screen door slam behind them.

Jake said, "You probably didn't notice, but Julia was paying a lot of attention to you. I think she might have a crush on you."

"If only she were Mary Bennett," John said. "But I think you're wrong. I think she likes you."

"I like Julia a lot," Jake said. "But I fear Luther. Luther seems to think Julia is his woman, and anyone else who shows Julia any attention takes his life in his hands. Our last boarder left, the one you're replacing, for fear Luther would beat him to a pulp."

"If you love this woman, Jake, then you should let her know and not be intimidated by this fool," John said.

"That boarder had shown some attention to Julia, and she seemed to like him. The next thing, Luther challenged the man to a fight. Luther made up some reason why he was mad at him. Well, you've seen how big Luther is, at least six feet six inches, and he's built like a cedar tree. He must weight two hundred and fifty pounds and his arms are like tree trunks. He's the foreman at the logging camp. Anyway, our boarder was so scared of Luther he just up and quit Nestlé and headed south towards California."

"If Luther gets in the way of your relationship with Julia then we will fight him together," John said.

Jake smiled. John enjoyed the sound of their footsteps echoing on the boardwalk. Off in the distance he could see the Nestlé Food Company buildings coming into view as they left the town behind and entered the spit of land that jutted out into Bandon's Bay. They passed by Nestlé's power plant building and heard the electric and steam engines rupturing the quiet of the morning. Just before entering the main Nestlé plant they passed by the elevated water tank. This tank was filled with water from a reservoir that was up in the mountains. Inside the plant, Robert Crowe was waiting for them.

"Good morning, Jake and John, glad to see you both and so prompt, too. Jake, are you a basketball player?"

"I like the game a lot. Why?" Jake said.

"John's already told me he was an outstanding basketball player at his high school in Portland. He's agreed to join our plant team. Can we count on you, too?"

"Yes sir, I would enjoy that," Jake said.

"Then be on the lookout for more players, because in October we will start putting the team together. The three of us will be the nucleus of that team. For now, let's get John acquainted with the factory, the rest of the employees, and his responsibilities."

The three of them walked to where Jake's main job was, the milk weighing station. This room was inside the plant within close proximity to both the front entrance and dock doors. They showed John the steps Jake went through in admitting the milk. One of those steps included assessing how much butterfat was in the milk. The richer the butterfat the higher the price the farmer was paid. Jake had many other responsibilities working in the weigh station.

From the weigh station, gleaming pipes pierced the wall and carried the incoming milk to the rest of the plant. John was dumbfounded by the way the pipes stretched in web-like fashion as they routed the milk from one station to the next. Bursts of steam exploded here and there and deafening steam-powered engines filled the air. As the two followed the pipes, Robert explained each process to John while introducing him to the plant personnel.

"Condensed milk averages 2.23 pounds of fluid whole milk to make one pound of evaporated milk," Robert said. "Once the cans are filled with milk they are sterilized and then packed into shook crates. The crates are taken to the warehouse to await shipment to San Francisco. Your job today will be loading these crates onto the incoming ship; also you will be unloading the ten gallon cans filled with milk from the stern-wheelers."

He introduced John to three men working in the warehouse area. One, Joe Tully, would be responsible for training John. John noticed at once that Joe was very friendly, and Robert said, "Joe will teach you the job and he is a very patient instructor. I'm sure you two will work well together." Robert then said, "Goodbye for now," and off he walked.

The first boat to come in was the stern-wheeler *John Wilde*. Joe explained the process of unloading the boat and how it was very important to get the ten-gallon milk cans deposited into the holding tanks as soon as possible. The unloading of the stern-wheeler took all morning and at noon the men ate lunch. After lunch, at about 1 p.m., a large steamship from San

Francisco arrived. Joe patiently instructed John on the unloading and loading techniques. This work lasted the rest of the day. Coming down the gangway, John, with sweat dripping from his body, wheeled the dolly stacked high with boxes to their designated locations. Then he wheeled the dolly back up the gangway piled high with heavy shook crates of condensed milk. His muscles ached with pleasure as he worked the freight. At 6 p.m. the work day came to a close.

Chapter 6

At 6:15 p.m., Jake and John walked towards Mrs. Smith's boarding house. They talked excitedly about starting up the basketball team in October. Jake told John of some possible recruits that worked in the factory. They both realized that their team was going to be something special. John could visualize Robert Crowe as a guard and leader, himself as the center, and Jake as the other guard, and he figured they needed only two more players as forwards to complete their team. They would also need some extra players for substitutes. They talked of playing neighboring towns and Bandon's high school. Before they knew it, Mrs. Smith's boarding house loomed just ahead of them.

John held the squeaky screen door open for Jake and then followed him into the house. The two loggers, Luther and Matt, were already seated at the dining table waiting for dinner to be served. In a booming voice Luther said, "Well it's about time! Get upstairs and wash up so we can eat dinner. Mrs. Smith has been holding supper until you two showed up." John looked at Luther and held Luther's menacing stare; it was Luther's eyes that finally dropped.

On their way upstairs, John said softly, "Jake, don't be afraid of Luther. Together we can handle him." John reminded himself that he could attempt almost anything especially while holding his magic charm: his father's watch. When they returned to the table, Julia and her mother started serving supper. It was another wonderful meal, and all the diners dove in. Again, there was little conversation, unless the slurp of hungry men shoving food into their mouths, the clink of silverware as it bounced off the porcelain plates, the thud of the glasses hitting the table, was "talk." John could smell the aroma of fresh coffee as it boiled in the kitchen. As the men finished their meals, Julia brought the coffee. As she poured coffee for Luther, he grabbed her wrist and said, "Julia, I think you want to go to the dance with me tonight." Julia, with her ever-present smile, turned red, but continued to pour coffee.

"No, I can't do that."

"You will have a good time if you go with me, and I promise to get you home before 10 p.m." Luther didn't take his hand off Julia's wrist until she glared at him.

Matt said, "Aw, go with the guy, Julia. If you were to go with him then he wouldn't be so mean at work." With that comment, Luther gave Matt a cold stare. Matt quickly followed with, "Luther is the best logging crew boss in the Coast Range mountains. Without him the logging company would go belly up. Why, he's saved me from being beat up two times. Julia, the guy thinks you are wonderful, so why not go out with him?"

"I have told Luther I will not go out with him. That is my final word on the subject," she said. She poured John's coffee then carried the used plates to the kitchen.

Luther, looking at no one, said aloud, "One of these days she will go with me and be damn glad she did, right Matt?"

"Sure thing, Luther, sure thing," and Matt rolled his beady eyes toward the ceiling. John could see that Luther was having a difficult time dealing with being turned down. His face was beet red and his furrowed brow became more pronounced as he looked around the room.

"I hope no one else in this room asks Julia out, because if they do they will be in a lot of trouble," Luther said. Luther's voice was very low, and John figured it was so Julia wouldn't hear from the kitchen. Both Luther and Matt looked at Jake and John, as if they wanted to provoke a fight.

John pulled out his watch and looked at it.

"What's that in your hand?" Luther said.

"My watch," John said.

"Let me see it."

"No," John said and put the watch back in his pocket. In a gentler voice Luther said, "I won't hurt it, let me see it."

John reconsidered, unsnapped the watch from his pants and handed it to Luther. Luther examined it and then he shoved it roughly into his own pocket. John stood immediately and his chair fell back, slamming on the floor with a loud bang. Luther stood too and both were staring at each other. Julia came back in the room.

"What's going on in here?" she said looking at the up-ended chair. Luther quickly pulled the watch out of his pocket.

"I was just looking at John's watch," Luther said, and he handed it back to him.

"John, let's go up to our rooms. I've had enough of this silly business," Jake said.

On their way up the stairs, Jake asked John if he wanted to go to the dance that night. "We might meet some girls."

John said, "Not tonight, Jake. I'm still getting settled in my room, but maybe next week." Later, John heard Jake as he walked down the stairs and went out the front door. He heard the screen door slam a few

minutes later, and he looked out the window to see
Luther and Matt going the same direction as Jake.

One of the amenities at Mrs. Smith's was that coffee
was kept hot on the stove until 9 p.m. every night. It
was about 8 p.m. when John went down stairs to get
a cup of coffee. Julia came out of her bedroom to join
him. John was pouring coffee and when he saw Julia,
he poured her a cup as well. They sat down at the
small kitchen table.

"Where is your mother?"

"She's in her room. My mother has been nipping
on moonshine. She gets it from an old high school
friend up in the hills. I'm afraid my mother has the
unwholesome habit of drinking a little too much
alcohol. She starts at about 4 p.m. every day. By the time
8 p.m. rolls around, she's usually drunk and asleep."

John responded, "That's too bad. I've heard of
people being controlled by whiskey like your mother. I
hope she will one day be able to break the habit." There
was an easy silence, punctuated by the steady ticking
of the kitchen clock. "Do you know Mary Bennett?"

Julia smiled. "We have been good friends since
grade school. Mary is engaged to Earl Jacobs, who is
off to college on the East Coast." John confessed his
admiration for Mary. Hearing Mary's name coupled
with Earl's made John jealous. Julia changed the subject.

Julia confided that Luther was getting more
aggressive in his approach to her. "The last boarder
left rather hurriedly, and I think it was because Luther
thought I had flirted with him. I really feel Luther
chased this man off. He had no right to. Luther thinks
he owns me and I haven't ever given him the idea
that I like him. John, he is becoming a lot bolder with
me. You saw him grab my wrist tonight. It's not the

first time, either. The last time he grabbed me like that, he tried to kiss me right here in the kitchen. He pushed me against the drain board and I kicked him in the shins. He let go and I ran into my bedroom and locked the door. He even tried to open the door. Jake came home right then, so Luther gave up. He's used to getting his way and is very strong. If it happens again, I have decided I will report him to the sheriff."

"You should have reported the incident the first time it happened, Julia. You can count on me and Jake to help if he acts like that again." John and Julia talked until about 9:30 p.m., and then decided to call it a night.

Once in bed, John fell fast asleep. Later he roused and heard Jake come in and go to his bedroom. A while later John was awakened again when the front door slammed shut. John opened his door so he could hear what was going on downstairs. He heard loud footsteps that seemed to go straight to Julia's bedroom door. He thought he heard someone, probably Luther, given the heavy tread, knock on Julia's door. He heard the sound of the doorknob, too, so John got up and dressed quickly. He roused Jake and the two of them went quietly down the stairs.

"Julia, Julia, won't you come out and have some coffee with me?" Luther tried the door again, this time harder. It was locked. Luther began pounding on the door, begging Julia to come out. He worked himself into an agitated state and managed to break open the door. Julia screamed. Luther rushed in and grabbed her, put his hand over her mouth and threw her on her bed. He was on top of her squirming body when John and Jake ran into the room. They pulled Luther off.

Luther sprang to his feet, ran past the two men and out the door with John chasing him. Just then,

Matt came in through the front door. He was drunk, and collided with Luther, then ended up on the floor, a confused look on his face. Luther regained his balance and turned on John. The two were nose to nose.

"I'm going to kill you for busting up my chance to be with Julia," Luther said. John knew Luther meant what he said. John could see the fire in Luther's eyes, saw his pulsating nostrils, and could see his muscled body throbbing with anger. Luther towered at least six inches over John. John was almost nudged off of his stance by the overbearing powerful brute, but John stood his ground and showed no fear in spite of Luther's enormous size advantage.

John said, "I want to speak to you outside."

Fully expecting to be in a fight, Luther said, "Let's go!" Luther led the way out the front door, Matt having rolled himself out onto the porch. Matt roused when the two men stepped over him. As John passed Jake, he whispered, "Go get the sheriff."

Once outside, Luther and John came face to face in Mrs. Smith's front yard. Light from the front door spilled out on the two combatants, with Luther shading the smaller John. John felt no fear, but in his anxiety his blood rushed through his veins like rapids on a river. The shaken Julia had emerged from her bedroom and out onto the front porch. She watched as Luther lunged forward and threw a right fist at John's face.

John, with the quickness of a cat, sidestepped the blow. Luther's body plunged forward and into a salal shrub, causing him to fall to the ground. By this time, Matt had recovered slightly and he picked up a vine maple walking stick that was leaning against the wall. He raised the cane and crept down the front porch steps. Julia stuck out her foot just then and Matt tumbled down the stairs face first; the cane fell at John's feet.

John picked up the stick and, as Luther was getting to his feet, John hit Luther across the side of his head. The blow was hard enough to cut into Luther's ear. Luther staggered from the blow. John swung a second time and delivered another blow and this time Luther went down hard. John immediately turned to face Matt who was still on the ground, not moving any more. John pulled Matt by the right leg over to where Luther lay.

About five minutes later, Jake and the Sheriff arrived in his Dodge. Both unconscious bodies were handcuffed and thrown into the caged rear end of the Dodge just like countless other drunks and criminals, and hauled off to jail.

Blakely The Heirloom

Chapter 7

Leaving Mary behind had been one of the hardest decisions Earl had ever made. Try as he might, he could not turn away from his need to explore the world, both in books and in deeds. He began his freshman year at Harvard while living at his Aunt Claudia and Uncle Jimmy's house in Cambridge. Earl's aunt and uncle had two children, Mark and Sarah. Mark was one year younger than Earl; Sarah was two years younger, and voluptuously mature for her age. Earl and his cousins became fast friends almost from his arrival in Cambridge, and when Earl was not at school or studying, it was a common sight to see the three on picnics, horseback rides, or walking together on the main streets of town.

In his letters home to Mary, Earl tried to describe his sense of closeness to his relatives. It was grand to finally meet them in person because all he had known of them were the pictures from his mother's photo albums. "My Aunt and Uncle are very hospitable," he wrote. "They serve me lucious meals and gave me a room upstairs that overlooks an orchard. I wish you could meet them. They are charming people, and one day you shall."

"My cousins," he continued, "are full of life and we have enjoyed many outings together. Mark, who is four inches taller than me, dreams of working on a windjammer and sailing around Cape Horn to the Pacific Ocean. My Aunt is terrified that he even thinks of such a voyage. Sarah is an accomplished musician playing classical music that soothes the soul. We have had great times together." And his letter ended as usual with, "I miss you terribly. Please write soon. Love, Earl."

Chapter 8
The Mermaids

Time passed and the little community of Bandon, Oregon, with its fourteen hundred and forty souls, busied itself with logging, fishing, mining, cheese making, and of course, making condensed milk at the condensary. The days were getting cooler as the fall of 1921 began; the wind seemed to be blowing all the time. The summer sun had gradually disappeared and with its departure clouds and fog moved in, shrouding the little community in an envelope of steely gray. It was late October.

John was dying to see Mary again. He had looked for her every time he went to town, but she wasn't to be found. He learned from Julia that she left school about 4 p.m. every weekday to catch the *John Wilde* home. On Tuesday, he talked his way out of work early. He saw Mary coming down Main Street heading for the docks, and he could barely believe his eyes. If anything, she was lovelier than he remembered.

"Mary!" She looked up from the arm-load of books she was carrying. " It's been a long time since I've seen you. How have you been?" he asked.

"I've been just fine. I hear about you all the time from Julia. She says you saved her life. She talks very fondly of Jake, too. Jake told her that you had been promoted to manager of the shipping department."

"I received a raise in pay also," John said with

pride. As they walked, it began to rain and John opened his umbrella and held it over Mary's head. He couldn't believe he was with her again; he was stunned by her natural beauty. He was cherishing every moment with her and felt a certain pride he had never known before. That Julia had spoken of him to Mary made him smile inwardly.

"Do you still have that watch you showed me on the boat?"

"I do," he said.

"I think of that inscription often. It's so true. To achieve anything in life one must persevere. Don't you agree?"

"Yes, Mary, I agree," John said.

Mary said, "I hear from Earl twice a week. I know that in order for him to graduate he must persevere and I must persevere also in waiting for him. I know he will come back when he finishes college."

At the mention of Earl's name John realized he didn't want to hear any more about Earl. "We are starting a Nestlé basketball team," John said. "We'll be practicing twice a week at your high school." They walked out onto the wooden dock and to the stern-wheeler's boarding plank. "There will be dances after the games. Do you think you would you like to go sometime?" John asked.

"I can't John, but thank you for asking," Mary said. As she walked up the boarding plank, she turned and waved, then vanished into the stairwell that led up to the passenger deck of the boat.

The next Friday night, the Nestlé men gathered at the high school gym for their first basketball practice. After the first hour or so, John called a halt to play and ask the team members to sit down on the bench because he had something to say to them. Once everyone was on the bench, John spoke, "Robert, I want you to play guard. I've seen you shoot the long shot and you're good at it. Besides you dribble the ball better than anyone. Jake, you will be the other guard. Your main job will be defense. Joe, you will play a forward position along with Ray. I will play center. Eldon and Frank, you guys will be the substitutes for now. From now on these are the positions we will play in practices and games." Robert raised his hand and waved a piece of paper. "Robert, what do you have there?"

"Well, this is from the head office." He stood up, and John thought he saw Robert blush as he cleared his throat. "Any basketball team representing Nestlé, the Swiss-owned company, must be named Mermaids."

"Do they think this is a bunch of women playing?" John asked.

Jake picked the joke up with, "I can see the headlines now: 'After milking the cows, the Mermaids uddered in a new era of basketball.'"

"Come on guys, I'm only reporting what the administration wants us to do. In order to have an official Nestlé team, we have to be named the Mermaids."

"I'm not going to be on any team called the Mermaids," Frank Bliss said.

"Come on Frank, we need you. It's just a name," Robert said. But Frank wouldn't change his mind and he walked off the court in a huff. Eldon stayed, but he looked confused. The rest—John, Robert, Roy, Joe, and Jake—joked some more about the new team name, Mermaids. They agreed it was silly, but basketball was worth a lot more than worrying about a name like Mermaids.

After practice, John, Robert, and Jake walked out

of the gym together. John told them he'd heard that the Dairymen's League was pressuring the farmers to sign five-year contracts. "That way, the dairymen who sign will not be able to sell their milk directly to Nestlé, and furthermore, the league claims they only want to help the dairyman get fair prices for their milk. They feel that an organization like the Dairymen's League can also check on Nestlé's weighing machines and butterfat testing. In other words, the league's presence would make sure the factory is being honest," John said.

"Did you read the article in the Bandon newspaper about that German dairyman? The league pressured him into signing one of those contracts and he can't even read English! He's suing," Jake said.

Robert spoke, "All I know is that the only way the dairymen are going to sell their milk to us is to do it directly. I know of some who have signed the contract and still sell their milk to us without the league's knowledge. In fact, I can tell you that this happens frequently."

John responded, "Sounds like a recipe for trouble all around."

"This is one of the reasons why Nestlé started this team. Nestlé wants good relations with our town, and they want to keep the dairymen happy so they won't sign with the league," Robert said.

The Mermaid's first game was scheduled with Bandon High School. The Bandon *Western World's* reporter, Ben Harris, reported:

> The Bandon High School's basketball team is one of the best teams the high school has had in a long time. The coach feels this will be a good practice game for his squad. He told me that his center was six feet five inches tall and could jump like a kangaroo. It will be very hard for other basketball teams to stop this young man. "We

have a tremendous advantage; there isn't another team around with this sort of size at the center position," and the coach feels his squad might even take the state championship. The coach told me that his team has been practicing the fundamentals of the two-handed set shot, the underhanded free throw, and working on their defenses, both the zone and man to man. The game is scheduled to be played at the high school gym Friday night at 7 p.m. After the game there will be a big town dance at the Oriental building on Fillmore Street.

As both teams warmed up in the Bandon High School gym Friday night, John desperately hoped that Mary would be in the crowd. He glanced up and searched the faces in the bleachers, but he couldn't find her. The referee blew his whistle and brought the two teams to the center of the court. At 7 p.m. sharp the referee threw the ball up in the air and the six-foot John immediately out-jumped his six foot five inch adversary and knocked the ball to Robert. Robert potted his half court set shot. The crowd was astonished by the way John out-jumped his taller opponent. Robert passed the ball with pinpoint accuracy. He would pass to John, and John would score with ease under and around the basket. Jake and the other Mermaids contributed on defense as John and Robert led the team to its first victory by beating the high school 50 to 22. As the town's people left the gym they raved about John's jumping and shooting.

Ben Harris, writing in the Bandon *Western World*, claimed the "Mermaids, with John Dowd as their center, was the best team this town had ever seen."

Blakely   The Heirloom

Chapter 9
Nestlé Plant Tour

Following the first game, the Mermaids challenged and beat all business-sponsored and nearby high school teams. The Mermaids looked unbeatable with John as their center. Every Thursday when the *Western World* came out, the front page always told of the Mermaids exploits, of how well John Dowd had played, and information about the next scheduled game.

John was very happy about the basketball team's success, and he knew the team helped to alleviate tensions between Nestlé and the league. The Nestlé plant had risen to the status of being the largest condensary in the United States and possibly the world. John felt as though he had contributed to his company's success. Yet in spite of this success, John still lacked the one thing he wanted most in life, and that was Mary.

That opportunity presented itself at Nestlé's plant tour. The *Western World* reported:

Nestlé administrators have decided to have a plant tour of their Condensary on Saturday. They invite all the region's dairymen, businessmen, and townspeople. They will have their stern-wheeler leave the Coquille dock at 8 a.m. Saturday and pick up all interested dairymen along its route to Bandon. Greeting the boat as it arrives at Bandon's docks will be the Bandon High School band

and Nestlé administrators. We are all looking forward to this special event.

When Saturday came, John and other Nestlé leaders waited as the stern-wheeler slowly moved into position to be tied to the dock. When the first person stepped off the gangway, the Bandon High School band began playing a series of rousing marches. John was pleased to see Mary and her parents getting off the boat with the other dairymen. The newly appointed Nestlé Superintendent, Robert Crowe, addressed the crowd:

"Ladies and Gentlemen before we begin our plant tour I would just like to thank all of you for coming this morning. We have a lot planned for you today. Our tour will be handled in this fashion: we have a few administrators and plant foremen that will lead groups. They will lead you through the plant and explain to you our process of making condensed milk and answer any questions you might have. At the end of the tour we have a lunch planned for you in our cafeteria. After lunch we will all go to our warehouse where our West Coast Supervisor, Mr. Teebs, will explain to you what the economic outlook is for the condensed milk business. And now, we will break up into small groups and begin our tour."

Mary and her parents were in a group of eight that John would lead. When the groups were organized they all marched off to the milk weigh-in site. John faced his group and said, "I am sure you are all aware of the importance of keeping your milking stations as sanitary as possible. Also, it is very important that you provide your cows with good quality feed, and water that is untainted. After the cows have been milked, the milk must be kept cool until it reaches our plant."

One farmer asked John to explain how Nestlé

determines the fitness of the milk for canning purposes. John explained the acid tests that were currently in use. Then John led the group into the main production room. Spread out before the visitors in a large high-ceilinged room was the production assembly line of gleaming pipes, large tanks, vats, and pans, with steam exploding in giant spurts. The workers, all dressed in white smocks, were positioned at different stations on the line. The noise in the room was deafening. John showed his group the cooling and filtering processes. "The milk is warmed in these large tanks and then it goes into this vacuum pan where the milk is condensed."

"How many employees does Nestlé have," a farmer shouted above the noise?

"One hundred twenty-five," John shouted back.

Mary was standing right in front of John, and over the noise she asked, "How many pounds of whole milk does it take to make one pound of condensed milk?"

John was delighted that she had asked him this question. "It takes about two point two-three pounds of milk to make one pound of condensed milk." John thanked Mary for her question. Mary's eyes lit up. Then, John led the group to the can-filling and sterilizing machines. Next, he guided the group through the chemistry lab, where Ray Wilkins was busy testing the newly-made canned milk, and then they passed through the vibrating power house with its ear-shattering steam engines. Finally, they ended up in the warehouse where Joe Tully was stacking shook crates, getting them ready for shipment to San Francisco, the last stop on the tour.

The groups then gathered in the cafeteria and went through the buffet line choosing food they wanted. With steaming food on their trays, the guests then sought out a place to sit at the tables and benches. John joined Mary and her parents at their table. John noted that the crowd became much quieter as they began eating lunch.

Mary's mother said, "John, thank you for leading our group. You seem very well versed in the production of canned milk." John nodded while biting into a roll.

"But you know this production process is not all that is happening in the condensed milk business. We have recently been confronted with league representatives putting a lot of pressure on us to join the Dairyman's League. We are really unsure of what to do at this point." Mary's father, Adam, nodded in agreement as his wife and John talked about the business. John looked at his watch and then said, "From what I understand, some dairymen belong to the league but still sell their milk directly to Nestlé. As of now they have chosen not to sue those dairymen."

Mary said, "The league contract states we have to sell our milk to the league, and then the league sells the milk to Nestlé. But if Nestlé won't buy from the league, the league is forced to sell our milk to the cheese-making businesses. We won't get paid for a long time. It's too long a process, all that waiting. When we sell to Nestlé, we get our money up front."

John had no idea Mary was so interested in her parents' business. As she spoke, John noticed the serious look on Mary's face, right down to her pouty lower lip. When she turned to speak again, a big beaming smile lit her face. John nearly lost his composure and sailed into another time zone only to be roused by Jake's elbow pushing into his back from a neighboring table and whispering, "John, Mr. Teebs is about to speak."

John could barely hear the remarks being made by Mr. Teebs. His mind was on Mary: what had happened to Earl? He'd heard that Earl's parents had left town, too. Adrift in these thoughts, he looked back at Mary and finally let the Superintendent's words through.

"The Bandon Condensary is the finest plant on the West Coast and quite possibly the world. We're equipped to handle 250,000 pounds of milk a day. We now take in most of the milk produced in Coos and Curry counties. Our company wants you to know we pay top prices in competition with the butter and cheese producers. We have $400,000 invested in this community and are not about to desert you. The only thing that we ask is that you sell your milk to us directly and not go through the Dairymen's League." Finally, Mr. Teebs concluded his speech, which also brought the day's festivities to an end.

John walked with Mary and her parents back to the *John Wilde* for the trip back up the river. "Would you go to the dance with me this Friday night after the basketball game?"

"I'd love to, John. I've read about you and how good a basketball player you are. I would like to see you play." Then with a certain authority in her voice she said loud enough for her parents to hear, "I will stay in town Friday after school, with Julia."

Her mother said, "John, thank you for asking Mary out. She has been very depressed for the last few weeks. Earl sent her a letter ending their long standing engagement. I really thought she would never come out of it, but thanks to you her spirits are revived."

"Oh, Mother, John's not interested in that news, please don't say any more." John's eyes brightened. At last, an opportunity to be with Mary!

Blakely

The Heirloom

Chapter 10
Earl Falls in Love With Another

Being with his cousins and going to college opened a whole new life for Earl. He had to study hard to keep up with his peers because the professors demanded high achievement in the classroom. When it came time to play, he really enjoyed the companionship of his cousins, Mark and Sarah. Away from the classroom, it was a time to enjoy life to its fullest. For the first several months, he did write Mary at least twice a week. Earl was still lonely. It was his first extended time away from home, and Cambridge couldn't be much farther from Bandon. He wanted someone close to talk to, and he missed the companionship Mary had given him. Mary hadn't just listened, she laughed, she questioned, and she really cared about the things Earl talked about.

It was a gradual thing, how Sarah filled the empty place left in Earl. She was intelligent, kind, and she possessed an irresistible natural beauty. Earl sensed she enjoyed his company, too.

The three cousins often scheduled picnic outings, but one day Mark got sick and couldn't go. Earl and Sarah decided to go without him. They made their way up on a hillside in a park next to a cemetery and with their picnic items spread out on a manicured lawn amid the fall colors, the two ate their lunch. Earl and Sarah teased each other incessantly. Earl sometimes wondered if it was their family heritage that allowed them to get along so well together. There were times though, when Earl knew his interest in Sarah was close to crossing the boundary between just being cousins, and that she was becoming a woman in his heart. He could barely take his eyes off the blond hair that fell to her hips. She was like that moment when a peach blossom bursts open in the spring.

After they had eaten, Sarah repacked the picnic basket. The sun was still high in the sky, and Earl was surprised it was so warm out. Their conversation had slowed some, and Sarah grabbed a handful of clover and tossed it into Earl's red hair. He pretended to be outraged and tried to rid his head of the clover. She tossed some more clover at him, and he lunged in her direction. Sarah's voice tickled his ears and before he knew what had happened, they had rolled together into the middle of the blanket, and Sarah was on top of him and they were embracing. He could not get enough of her blue eyes, and he could feel every inch of her voluptuous body as she lay above him.

Her pleasant scent enveloped Earl in a cloud of lemons and vanilla. He rolled her over and could feel her heart as it pounded beneath him. The sweet smell of her body teased his nose and his eyes gazed into hers. Earl tried to take his eyes away from Sarah's but couldn't. Her eyes were like a magnet and he could not look away. Unable to resist any longer, Earl's lips slowly descended on Sarah's waiting mouth. Earl felt Sarah's soft warm lips and a tongue that teased. When they parted from their embrace, Earl looked at Sarah in a new way, no longer cousins but something deeper. They hadn't said a word to each other yet.

Lying on their backs and looking up at the sky Sarah finally let words enter the silence. "We mustn't do this. What of Mary?" Earl felt his heart lurch at

Mary's name. It wasn't that he didn't love her, but here he was with Sarah, and he simply couldn't deny this day, this time.

"Earl, I've longed to kiss you ever since you arrived. There! I said it. Are you mad at me because I said it? This could never have happened had Mark been along. I'm so happy he didn't come today. Did you enjoy the kiss?"

"Yes, Sarah, I did." And they turned on their sides facing each other and kissed again. Earl felt he was betraying Mary yet Sarah offered a new and interesting relationship. On the one hand Sarah was as beautiful and wonderful as Mary. He had promised his love to Mary, but it seemed like years ago. As their lips parted this time, Earl said, "Maybe you're right, we shouldn't do this." Sarah looked away and her body heaved as she sobbed. "Sarah, please don't cry." When she turned her head around Earl saw a passionate woman who was desperately in love with him. It was an irresistible look and Earl collapsed into her waiting arms.

Earl wrestled with his love for Mary and his new appreciation for Sarah. He knew Mary, but Sarah was so new, a discovery. Yes, he was lonely, but this was something deeper. Sarah seemed to understand his inner thoughts in a way no one else did. He didn't know why. Yet, as Earl pondered what Mary would think, he knew deep down that what he was doing was wrong, that he was committing a grievous misjudgment. For some unexplainable reason he couldn't stop himself.

The sun was bright as it moved across the sky, but then it reached the tree tops and the day started to darken. Earl and Sarah had stayed closely embraced, as if in a magical spell, for most of the day. As the lengthening shadows crept up on their bodies, they reluctantly let go of each other; it was time to leave.

They gathered up their picnic items and Earl carried most of the load. Then, amid the last vestiges of a beautiful fall day, they walked hand in hand down the grassy slope.

When they returned home, both tried to keep what had happened a secret. Earl went to his room and tried to study, he even tried to write Mary a letter, but gave up on both and lay on his bed thinking. He couldn't get Sarah's sweet presence out of his mind; the harder he tried the more he craved to be with her. He opened his door to go downstairs and saw Sarah's lovely shape already ascending, and when their eyes met they again embraced. They sought out a little hidden alcove where they kissed and petted until they heard Mark's cough as he was coming upstairs. Sarah dashed toward her room and Earl returned to his room.

Earl was beginning to fear what his Uncle and Aunt might think. When they had returned from their business outing Aunt Claudia prepared dinner for the family. Uncle Jimmy paced as he waited for supper. The smell of fried chicken filled the house, and at 6 p.m. Claudia called Jimmy and all the children to the table. There were only four for dinner, as Mark was still feeling poorly and decided not to eat with the family.

"How was your picnic today?" Aunt Claudia asked.

"We had a great time except that Sarah is so slow sometimes I wish she had a bicycle so she could keep up with me."

"A bicycle! I think not!" chided Sarah. "Maybe you need to slow down. Remember your legs are longer then mine. Pass the green beans."

Uncle Jimmy asked how Earl was doing at Harvard.

"Just fine, in fact I am getting excellent marks in all of my classes. I never realized there was so much to learn, I feel that this four years will really be worth the time."

Earl's gaze then settled on Sarah's and they both smiled.

Earl suspected that Mark was aware that he and Sarah were having an affair. He knew Mark didn't have to be a genius to come to that conclusion, as Earl and Sarah had stopped including Mark in their many outings. Earl was certain, though, that Mark would never betray them, so Earl and Sarah continued deceiving everyone accept Mark. Earl's aunt and uncle were completely oblivious and had no inkling of what was going on. Earl and Sarah planned to wed after Earl's graduation from college.

As the weeks passed, Earl came to the difficult conclusion that it was time to write Mary and tell her that their engagement was off. It was the hardest thing for Earl to do. How could he tell Mary, his childhood friend and lover, what was happening? But tell her he must, because they had always been honest with each other. He did not want to deceive Mary because in spite of what was happening, he still adored her. He did not ever want to lose their friendship and fervently hoped they would be able to continue to write to each other, even though now they would be separated from their childhood commitment of marriage. There was no easy way to say such disappointing words.

Sarah insisted that Earl write to Mary as soon as possible.

Dear Mary,

It is with considerable hardship that I write you this letter. I hardly know where to begin or end. I dream of you incessantly and cherish the wonderful childhood we shared together, so please believe me when I say this: I miss you terribly. When I left Bandon I left with the best intentions of fulfilling our youthful dreams, but now other developments have happened. I regretfully and respectfully want you to know that it will be impossible for me to carry out those dreams. Over the last few months I have fallen in love with Sarah. We plan to wed as soon as I graduate from college. Please forgive me. I pray you will not exclude me from your life. I want to know what is happening to you and fervently wish we can continue to correspond.

Love,

Earl

Earl received Mary's reply a month later.

Dear Earl,

It was with tears dripping down my face that I read your letter. It took me weeks to recover. If it had not been for my parents and my daily chores, I would have ended my own life. I had a hard time envisioning life without you in my future. But now I must move on away from what was once very precious to me.

Julia has been talking about a friend of hers that lives in her mother's boarding house and whom I have met. He really wants to see me, and in fact you met him on the dock the day before you left for the East Coast. His name is John. Because of you I had discouraged any outside relationships but now I have decided to meet with him.

I, too, will always cherish the past we shared together. But now I must move into the future! I wish you the best in your new relationship. Even though I am so very disappointed in you, I still would like to continue our correspondence.

Love,

Mary

As Earl read the words Mary had written, he immediately felt a jealousy he had not experienced before. He remembered the young man on the dock and how he had felt when he saw Mary holding his hand, and that feeling immediately returned. Earl felt that a part of his life had just slipped out of his fingers, maybe a part he was too fast to discard. He desperately loved Mary yet now he had committed himself to a new future; he wondered if it was as secure as the one he had had with Mary. Had he made a mistake? And would that mistake erode the charmed life he had thus far been able to lead? No matter, he just could not resist the warmth and beauty of Sarah, his uncle's daughter.

Every Sunday, Uncle Jimmy and Aunt Claudia would take the entire family to church services. They went to a small non-denominational church on the outskirts of town. The family always sat in a pew towards the rear. The pastor had a loud vibrating voice that could be heard even in the belfry atop the church. On this particular Sunday after the hymns had been sung and the pastor had given most of the sermon, this week on Christ's rebirth, he concluded the sermon with a warning to his parishioners on the sinful act of incest.

Standing at the pulpit, high above his congregation, his voice rang out as if through a megaphone. He told the congregation, "In the few minutes I have left, I would like to discuss the many hardships that befall people who engage in the despicable act of incest. Daughters who are abused by their fathers are permanently scarred for the rest of their lives. Yes, right here in this church we have members who have indulged in this terrible act. They want God to forgive them. But only God in his merciful goodness can help these poor souls. I can guarantee you that these people are some of saddest people I have ever met. They despise themselves for their weaknesses and the harm they have caused. Sometimes children are the result of these relationships. These children are at risk of being mentally inadequate to deal with the many hardships of life. Of course most of you know this and this subject needs little explanation here.

"But, it has also come to my attention, recently, of another child born to a relationship of cousins. His name was Meriwether Lewis, the famous adventurer that traveled across the country with Clark to the Pacific Ocean. I read that Lewis was mentally unbalanced. This condition led him to commit suicide by shooting himself to death in September of 1809. I'm telling you all this because I'm hoping that incestuous relationships like this will not develop in your families. You must do everything you can to prevent them from happening."

Earl saw the color drain from Sarah's face, and he could see her fight to hold back tears. She kept looking away from her parents for fear they might see a tear. To Earl it felt as if he had been hit by a cannon ball. Never in his life had a preacher spoken in such harsh language to Earl's own life.

The final hymn was sung and the parishioners filed out of the church into a sun-filled afternoon.

On their way home Aunt Claudia said, "Fathers who commit such acts should be hanged. It is unholy and very harmful." Uncle Jimmy nodded in agreement. This new revelation was having an eye-opening effect on Earl and Sarah. Mark was in between them in the back seat of the car. The secret lovers gazed out the windows apparently in deep thought. When they arrived back home Earl and Sarah excused themselves for a walk before dinner.

"I think it's hogwash. Two of my best friends have cousins for parents and they are perfectly happy and just as smart as can be. Who knows, this Meriwether Lewis business may be a hoax. There are many mentally unbalanced people in this world. Oh Earl, please don't let this interfere with us."

Earl was thoughtful for a long while then said, "We must consider the possibilities of having children and how they would be affected if we were to marry. You want to have children, don't you?"

"Of course, I do, your children, and they will all be fine." Sarah began to cry. Earl put his arm around her and held her close as they came to a stop. He tenderly kissed her. "We must get back, they're probably holding dinner for us."

A few days later Jimmy and Claudia invited the two young people into their parlor and closed the heavy sliding door behind them. Uncle Jimmy began. "Before we talk I'd like both of you to read this letter from Earl's mother." Earl read it first then handed it to Sarah.

Dear Sister Claudia,

Unfortunately, there is a terrible situation going on under your very noses. That relationship was revealed to me by Mary, Earl's childhood sweetheart. Earl ended his engagement with Mary, saying he was going to marry Sarah as soon as he graduated from college. We are very upset about these circumstances. Tom is going to quit his job here and we will move back to Cambridge where Tom should be able to find another bank job. We are planning to buy a house there and we will provide living quarters for our son until he graduates. For now it is of the utmost importance we do everything in our power to end this evil relationship.

Love,

Betty

Uncle Jimmy finally said, "Last week we all attended a church service where the Pastor talked about the consequences of incestuous behavior. It is unfortunate, but true, that children from such a union could be mentally damaged. I ask you to remember the pastor's example, Meriwether Lewis. Thank God, children are not in the offing from your relationship. You two are first cousins and the continuance of your improper relationship could result in your children being deranged, malformed or God only knows what could happen. Earl, your folks were very upset to learn about your indecent relationship with our daughter. It is not only your fault, but Sarah's as well. You both must take the responsibility for the acts you commit. Claudia and I implore both of you to come to your senses. Face up to this unfortunate mistake and set your lives in a proper direction so you will be spared the embarrassment of unnecessary hardships.

"Claudia and I have decided that you both will be allowed one last private meeting to discuss what we have said. From that time on Sarah will make known to us her location at all times and the two of you will never be alone again. Earl, your folks will be here soon to take up residency and you will live in their home until you graduate. That is about all we have to say on this matter and we both hope and pray that you two will come to your senses. May God forgive you."

Sarah began to cry. Earl knew how hard this had been for her, holding it all in and just waiting for it to all end, as he knew it would. He saw Sarah's face covered in tears and it broke his heart. Through the tears Sarah said, "I cannot stop loving Earl. We plan to marry when he graduates. I will not change these plans for you or anyone!"

Earl was shattered by the letter from his parents, but somehow he had expected it. Sarah rose from her chair and rushed from the room, sobbing loudly as she climbed the stairs. Earl knew it would be very hard to break off with his cousin whom he adored, but the impact of what Uncle Jimmy had said made sense and there just was nothing else he could do. Earl had made a grave miscalculation, and because of it he knew he would lose not only Sarah but Mary, too. He vowed to himself to end this relationship with Sarah, to make amends with his parents and his aunt and uncle, and then seek forgiveness from Mary.

Blakely   The Heirloom

Chapter 11

Moonshine

John knew that Mary had suffered a lot at the loss of her beloved Earl. As her mother had said, Mary had been depressed for a month. More than anything else, John wanted to cheer Mary up, hoping it would cause her beautiful smile to return. He could hardly wait for Friday's work day to end, because that's when Mary had agreed to go to the basketball game with him and spend the night at the boarding house as Julia's guest.

When Jake and John came home from work, all five had dinner together. The dinner was a special occasion because not only were John and Mary enjoying each other's company for the first time, but a romance was blossoming between Julia and Jake. John raised his glass and said, "Here's a toast to our basketball victory this evening!" Everyone toasted and cheered.

"Here's to a wonderful dance," Julia raised her glass for the next toast, and there was another round of "Cheers." Mrs. Smith's toast, "Please remember to be home by twelve," was not so enthusiastically received. John enjoyed the festive atmosphere that Mrs. Smith was trying to create. He had noticed that she had delayed her customary drinking and sensed she was waiting for a later time. As they finished the meal, Mrs. Smith brought in fresh apple pie. There was little left of the pie by the time they had to leave for the game. The two couples left the house hand in hand, and Mrs. Smith nibbled at the last piece of pie crust after the screen door had slammed shut.

They entered the gym through two big doors. Bleachers were set up on each side of the court. The Nestlé's rooting section was filled with fans from the town of Bandon. The bleachers on the east side of the court were about half full of people from Port Orford. John was excited at seeing the town bleachers full. He heard his name called out, and some cheers as he walked down the court. John and Jake ushered the two women to seats in the Bandon section and then went to the team's dressing room.

John held his nose pinched as he walked into the dressing room. "What's that smell in here? Robert put your shoes back on!" The rest of the players imitated John and held their noses too. Robert laughed. The dressing room had metal lockers and two long benches. It was a room that had served many sweaty bodies. The players were sitting on the benches, most of them ready for the game, but a few were relacing their shoes.

Robert said, "All kidding aside, this team will be the toughest we have faced all year. They have won all of their games. Most of their players are Coast Guard recruits. Even with our superstar John here, we will have a tough time."

Jake said, "I'm from Port Orford and I know that the Coast Guard Unit there enlists only the best men for their crew. They are physically fit and very athletic. Be ready for a competitive game."

John said, "These guys are famous, too."

"And the reason these guys are famous," Robert said "was because just last week they saved three lives off the point of Cape Blanco. That's why we have such a big visitor section tonight. Port Orford residents have come here tonight in support of their famous team."

"We are going to have to play tough defense," John said. "Jake that means you are going to have to keep your mind focused on the game and not on Julia in the stands."

"Not only Jake, but you too, John," Robert said. "Jake, your parents were here earlier looking for you. Since it is almost game time, you will have to see them after the game. Let's get out there and warm up."

After the teams went through their warm up exercises, the referee blew a loud whistle and the starting five from both teams assembled for the center jump. Dwarfing John was the big six foot four Port Orford center. The referee stood between the two men and threw the ball up, starting the game. The Bandon crowd cheered as John out jumped the opposing center, knocking the ball to his guard, Robert. Robert shot a long set shot that swished through the net. The Mermaids were up by two. The referee brought the ball back to the center of the court and again John out-jumped his taller foe and Robert repeated on another basket. The Mermaids were up by four.

For the rest of the first half, John dominated at the center jump and rebounding. However, the scrappy guardsmen were no pushovers. Their superb ball handling and precision shooting kept them in the ball game for the first half. Much to their credit, they fought back, and by the end of the first half the score was tied at twelve. In the second half, John and Robert were just too much for the Port Orford team, as between the two of them they scored the next ten unanswered points with Robert connecting on his long shots and John hitting on his short shots around the key. When the guardsmen decided to concentrate their defense on Robert and John, the ball was thrown to Jake and he made two excellent top-of-the key scores. The final score was Mermaids 26, Port Orford 18.

The spectators spilled out onto the gym floor congratulating the players, and Jake was able to talk to his parents. "John, Robert," Jake said, "come over here. I want you to meet my parents." Jake introduced both John and Robert to his mother and father.

"We can't stay long," Jake's father said, "our ride is leaving soon." The three friends and team returned to the odorous dressing room. After dressing, Jake and John said good bye to their team members and went to find their girl friends. The four left the gym together and followed the crowd, the lively salt air whipping through their clothing and hair. The crowd was heading for Oriental Hall on Fillmore Street. Oriental Hall was a huge barn-like structure with apartments on the second story; some said the upstairs was a bordello.

The main floor had high ceilings and there was plenty of room for the dancers and the Coquille volunteer band. A big refreshment table was at the entry and the band was at the other end of the room. People mingled at the big table drinking punch and eating little prepared sandwiches. Groups of girls stood along the wall on one side of the room, and groups of boys stood along the wall on the opposite side, and they all watched as the dancers took up the space in the center of the room.

Mary, with a cup of punch in her hand said, "I know the violinist. I've seen him in Coquille many times. He's really good and usually plays fast and lively tunes." John thought it was about time he learned how to dance, so he grabbed Mary's hand and led her out on the dance floor and then tried to follow what every one else was doing. It wasn't long until he was dancing with the best of them. He found in Mary a lively partner who was able to transfer the beat of the music through her hands to his. Her natural rhythm helped him learn how to do the right steps.

John couldn't believe his eyes. "Look," he said to Mary, "Jake and Julia are doing a dance in front of everyone." The entire assemblage watched as Jake and Julia took the center of the room and performed as if they were professionals. At the end of their routine, Jake bowed and wiggled his ears, and Julia curtsied, her plump hands on her skirt.

The dancing and festive atmosphere was being enjoyed by all. John could tell some of the attendees were enjoying it a little too much; they were becoming tipsy and loud. As John and Mary danced, some of the dancers would bump and jostle them about. Some actually lost their balance and fell to the floor. Jake told Mary and John, "It's the moonshine. A few people are drinking way too much. They get it from this guy, Burt. He's outside, hiding in the bushes."

Even though these few people were somewhat disruptive, it didn't seem to bother the two couples from Mrs. Smith's boarding house; they were having a great time. About midway through the evening, John recognized two drunks coming through the big entry doors, Luther and Matt. They staggered in side by side, with Luther being very loud and obnoxious.

"I want to see the famous basketball player outside right now!" Luther bellowed. It was clear they had been drinking heavily and their loud raucous behavior was disturbing everyone. Luther spotted John immediately and approached him with his fists raised.

The band stopped playing and almost everyone in the room turned their attention to Luther and Matt.

"I have some unfinished business I want to settle with you," slurred Luther.

Matt, bushy haired, bearded, beady-eyed, and only five foot two standing erect, mimicked the same words, and danced around the room with his fists raised, but was careful not to get too far from his oversized logger friend and protector.

"If you refuse to come outside, then I'll get you right here," and Luther swung at John, missing badly and falling to the floor under the refreshment table. When he tried to get up he knocked over the table, which sent punch and sandwiches all over the floor.

Fortunately, the sponsors of the dance had providentially hired three big loggers, every one of them even bigger than Luther, to be on hand for just such an occasion. The three bouncers immediately landed on Luther and Matt and roughly tossed the two drunks out onto the street.

"If you come back inside we will call the sheriff and have you arrested," one logger said.

"Won't they ever stop bothering us?" Julia said.

"The only way is when they're put in prison where they belong," Jake said.

The mess the two intruders had created at the refreshment table was cleaned up and the band played another lively tune. The dance returned to the festive affair it had been.

The two couples resumed their dancing, only to be interrupted moments later by a neighbor of Mrs. Smith, Mrs. Norton, who was looking for Julia. When she found Julia she gave her a note.

"Julia, would you please buy me a jug of whiskey from Burt, for I have run out of whisky at home." Mrs.

Norton was gone when Julia looked up. Julia was exasperated and showed the note to her friends. "I was really hoping that my mother would stop drinking so much moonshine." "I'll help you find Burt," Jake told Julia. John and Mary said they would help too.

Once outside they found one of the heavy drinkers slouched against the building, "Burt's over there in those bushes," he told Jake. It appeared to John that Burt was getting ready to leave as they approached. Julia showed Burt the note her mother had written.

"Darn, I just ran out of my supply, Julia, but if you and your friends want to follow me to my brewing spot up near Ferry Creek Dam I can get you that jug."

The clouds had disappeared and the full moon glowed brightly, lighting up the night as if it were day. The four decided to follow Burt. They walked along a rough slippery trail that followed a raised wooden water trough that led to Ferry Creek Dam. The raised water trough funneled water from Ferry Creek Dam to Nestlé's condensary. John could hear the water as it sloshed overhead and felt the salal shrubs and blackberry brambles as they brushed against his calves and thighs.

Burt said, "Stop here for a minute. Shhhh!!! I thought I heard something. That revenue agent has been nosing around recently and I hope he is not following us. Ah, probably just the wind," and the group continued on.

Julia purchased a jug of whiskey and the four started back down the trail to town. Burt had aroused John's suspicions as to someone following them, but he couldn't see anything to confirm his feeling. If someone was following them, he was certainly clever because it was hard to hide in this moonlight.

Jake and Julia led the way down, stopping now and again to hug and kiss. John kissed Mary for the first time. He experienced the thrill of Mary's warm body close to him. It was the sweetest moment of his life. Parting, they followed Jake and Julia, talking in low whispers as they neared Mrs. Smith's boarding house.

John was caught off guard as Luther and Matt sprang out at them. The unsuspecting Jake took a brass knuckle punch to the mouth and nose that knocked him flat. John felt Matt trying to tangle up his arms and John's instinctive reflexes instantly threw Matt for a somersault. As John recovered from Matt's interference, Luther jumped him and threw right punches with the brass knuckles one after the other. John dropped to the ground losing consciousness. Julia stashed the jug in the bushes and then quickly jumped on Luther along with Mary. Matt aided Luther by pulling the women off his back. Finally, Luther stood over John's body and kicked him in the ribs.

Seeing John's helpless body on the ground, Luther reached his hand into John's watch pocket, but the pocket was empty. Luther saw the watch clenched in John's fist. Mary lunged at Luther and he caught her by the shoulders and slammed her to the ground. Luther tried to pry John's watch from his death-like grip. Before he could break the grip of John's fingers, Luther was grabbed around the neck from behind by the revenue agent. Luther blacked out. Matt, his hands full with fending off the women saw the revenue agent coming at him. He panicked and fought his way through the women, fleeing for the woods.

As Matt fled, the revenue agent yelled, "Halt or I'll shoot!" Matt kept running. The bullet hit his right shoulder but he kept on running. The revenue agent decided not to pursue Matt but instead concentrated his energies on making sure Luther could no longer threaten anyone. The agent handcuffed and hog-tied Luther. He then checked John and Jake to make sure they were still breathing and told the women to take care of them until he returned with the sheriff.

The women rushed to their boyfriends' sides and tried desperately to revive them. Jake was the first to come to, his nose bleeding and his lip badly cut. John finally roused too, his face bloodied in the nose and mouth, and blood trickling from his ear. His ribs ached and throbbed with pain. Jake was the first to stand, and then John, with a pained effort, stood up. They stayed with the unconscious Luther until the sheriff arrived.

The agent was in the lead as he brought the sheriff to the scene of the ambush. The sheriff opened his log book and made notes of the many charges that would be filed against Luther.

"Luther and Matt not only attacked you folks, but they broke into two businesses on Main Street before going to the dance. Luther knifed a bystander and the man nearly died. Doc Armstrong is looking after him. The charges against Luther will be attempted murder, assault, unlawful entry into a building, and theft. If he's convicted, it could be a long time before Luther gets out of jail," the sheriff said.

Both Jake and John thanked the agent for his timely appearance. The agent said, "We will look for Matt tomorrow. I'm sure I hit him, so I don't think he will get very far." Luther was shoved into the sheriff's caged auto and both sheriff and agent drove off. Julia retrieved the jug and John and Jake, aided by the girls, hobbled to the boarding house.

The next day while John was at Doc Armstrong's office, the revenue agent found him and said, "This morning, the sheriff and I went to the reservoir to bust up Burt's still operation, but when we got there, we didn't find a thing. Burt and all his equipment had vanished, poof, disappeared. Next, we searched for Matt and couldn't find him, either. It was a disappointing day."

Bleeding profusely and in pain, Matt had climbed up the forested hill that led away from Bandon, finally falling down to rest under a huge cedar tree. Next to the large tree was a creek and not far from the creek was the hidden campsite of a Coquille Indian couple and their infant son. Matt fell to the ground with a thump. Hearing the thud, the Indian couple found Matt unconscious. Over the next two months they nursed Matt back to health. Matt would never be able to use his right arm again; it would always hang limply at his side.

Chapter 12
Romance Blooms

Luther was in jail and headed to the state prison. Matt had vanished into thin air, and John hoped he was dead someplace in the woods. Mary helped nurse John's wounds after the ambush, but no amount of care could heal him in time for the Mermaids last game of the season. The last game was against the Deaf Mutes of Portland. The Bandon *Western World* headlined their article:

Mermaids to Play the Unbeaten Portland Team "Deaf Mutes" on Friday

The Portland team, learning of Nestlé's unbeaten record, challenged them to a game. The Deaf Mutes are also unbeaten in 20 outings and the contest should be a thrilling spectacle.

Two days were left before the big game. At their last practice in the high school gym, the Mermaids seemed at a loss as to how they would confront the Mutes without John's participation. Jake and Robert wanted John to play, but he said, "My ribs are just too sore, there's no way I can be ready by Friday night. My whole midsection is bandaged, plus the doctor said I might risk permanent injury if I played. I'll be there to cheer you on, but this time you are going to have to win without me."

"These guys are good," Jake said. "Ben Harris has

talked with Portland sports writers and claims the team is made up of deaf players. They were organized by a deaf man who learned how to play in a private school. They've beaten some big Portland business-sponsored teams."

"In that event, we have little choice as to how we will play the game," Robert said. "We will have to take long shots and hope that we can score."

"The whole town will be here for this game and we are without our best player," Jake lamented.

"We'll just have to do the best we can," Robert said. The team left practice that evening with their spirits down. The only good thing about the upcoming game for John was that he would be able to see Mary again. And after school, Mary would spend the night at the boarding house as she had done the week before.

Friday night arrived and the two couples were seated at the dining table for dinner. Mrs. Smith was a little tipsy, but she had managed to serve a decent dinner. She allowed Julia to enjoy the social get-together entirely; excusing her from the chores of helping with dinner and cleaning up afterwards. Mrs. Smith brought the diners their different entrees, making her way in and out of the kitchen's swinging door. Everyone knew that in between bringing the food she would sneak to her bedroom and drink from her jug.

After the meal, Julia went into the kitchen to see if she could help her mother do the dishes. Jake had some things to do before they left and went upstairs. John and Mary were left alone at the table.

"I haven't heard from Earl since that last letter ending our engagement. I hope he is all right," Mary said. John's hand went instinctively for his watch. Even though Julia had told him that Mary really liked him and felt flattered that he asked her out, every time he heard Earl's name he would get really angry. It was all he could do not to shout.

"I'm sure he is OK," John said. He could feel the pain in his jaw as he clenched back his anger.

"Have you noticed that Julia and Jake are almost engaged?" Mary said.

"Yes," John said, "Jake told me that he loves Julia and I think the feeling is mutual."

Julia and Jake came back into the room and they all decided to leave for the game. "I know my mother is probably way past tipsy, but there is nothing I can do about it," Julia said. John pushed opened the squeaky door, the couples headed off to the game.

Mary and Julia went to the town's rooting section, and John and Jake went to the dressing room. John said, "This will be the starting line up: Eldon will have to play center tonight. Joe and Ray will play forwards and Jake and Robert the guards."

"Let's go with this game plan," Robert said. "Every time we get the ball we will stall, passing as much as possible and shooting only when we get a clear unguarded shot. We will play a man-to-man defense. Let's go out there and win this game for John." John, taking up his cue, cheered his teammates on with a rousing, "You can do it, guys!" Over the next hour, however, John's fears were realized as the Mermaids lost 15 to 45. He didn't know if it would have made a bit of difference if he'd been playing either. Those guys were very good players.

John was proud of what the team had accomplished during the season with 20 wins and one loss. The team had helped John in two important ways: it had enhanced his friendship with Robert and Jake, and it had helped him secure the beginnings of a relationship with Mary—all wins in John's book.

"You guys may have lost this one game but remember, we had a great season," John said in the dressing room after the game. They all shook hands. Some left the room, but the final three were John, Robert and Jake.

Robert told his friends. "I want you guys to be the first to know that this afternoon I was informed by the Nestlé Corporation that I have been promoted to general manager of three plants in southern California. The Bandon plant will have a new superintendent and he should be in place by the end of the month. I leave next week for California. I hate to leave this place, because I have enjoyed our friendship like none other I have known. But I must accept this opportunity for a better position and more money with the company. One thing is certain, some day I'll be back."

John was saddened by the news. Robert was his best friend. He knew Robert was ambitious and there simply was no question about him not taking a better position; he must. He remembered the times the three of them worked with Jake trying to learn about the Coast Guard.

"I'm going to teach you all I know about the Coast Guard. My father taught me well," Jake had said. While rowing a canoe out into the ocean Jake would yell, "Tip her over!" Once in the cold water Robert and John were shown the proper way to return the boat to an upright position. "OK, climb back in," Jake would shout. He showed and taught them how to use other Coast Guard boats. "This is no business for sissies," he would say. Some times he would demand one of them jump into the water and then paddle off and he'd yell, "Swim over to the boat." As the swimmer neared, Jake would instruct John or Robert to paddle away from the swimmer. "You guys are going to have to be good swimmers to join the Coast Guard." John didn't think much about it at the time but knew these adventures tightened the bonds of friendship between the three young men.

John and Jake shook Robert's hand and wished him good luck as they all left the dressing room. The bad news of Robert's departure wasn't going to spoil the evening that John and Jake had planned. Joining in with the spectator crowd they headed towards Oriental Hall, and once again entered through the large doorway—a large ten foot wooden door on casters that had been slid open. This doorway was big enough for a horse and wagon to enter. Everything was as it had been the week before. The refreshment table, the Coquille band, the dancers, even the secret moonshine sales were going on outside. John was happy he was here at this dance with Mary.

He was having the best time of his life, and hoped Mary was too. From Mary's expression, he had a hard time deciphering what she was thinking. When the dance was over, John and his friends returned to the boarding house. Julia looked in on her mother.

"She's sound asleep," Julia said.

The young people were unburdened by parental restraints as the young men escorted the girls to their rooms. At the doorway to Mary's bedroom, John kissed her. The kiss lasted long enough for Mary to ease her door open. While still in an embrace, the two entered the room and shut the door behind them.

Once inside, John sat next to Mary on her bed. They cuddled together with John's arm draped around Mary's fragile shoulder. "I shouldn't allow this John; I love you so much that I can't bring myself to tell you to leave." John did not want to leave either. This was the moment John had longed for, alone with his arms around the person he felt closest to in the whole world. As John felt Mary's soft lips press against his their bodies rolled back on the bed. John gently removed Mary's blouse and tenderly felt her breasts; Mary unbuttoned John's shirt, exposing his bandaged ribs, but for John there was no pain only the rapture of the moment. As they fondled and kissed, they both slowly undressed and worked their way under the covers. This close and intimate union lasted well past midnight. Around 3:00 a.m., John woke up and realized he had better return to his room before Mrs. Smith should discover them. John grabbed his clothes, kissed Mary as she slept, and tiptoed across the hall to his bedroom. As he opened his door, he heard Jake coming up the stairs. Both men quietly acknowledged the other as they went to their rooms with out a word.

Chapter 13

The following Monday John took some time off work to walk Mary to the stern-wheeler. Mary had walked from school to Main Street when John met up with her. They walked hand and hand through the business district of town towards the docks.

"Do you know what happened while we were at the dance?" Mary asked. John didn't know.

"A Dairymen's League representative visited with my parents Friday night. He persuaded them to sign a five year contract. I read the contract over and it expressly forbids them to sell their milk directly to Nestlé."

John said, "Many a dairy farmer has done the same thing, but sells their milk to us anyway."

"I don't understand; if it's against the contract isn't it against the law for them to do that?" Julia asked.

"Yes, that's true, but so far the league hasn't sued anyone yet," John said.

"My father thought it was a brilliant business decision because now he can sell his milk secretly to Nestlé and sell whatever milk is left over to the cheese making businesses through the league."

"I agree with you, Mary, he should never have signed the contract." They walked out on the dock to where the steamer was tied up. They said their goodbyes and Mary walked up the boarding plank.

Chapter 14
Letter from Earl

By the time his parents arrived in Cambridge, Earl had managed to clear up the situation with Sarah and tried hard to make amends with his aunt and uncle. His parents found a house to buy and Tom found a good bank job. Earl moved in with his parents and continued to study at Harvard. But, Earl's mother Betty had caught the flu while riding on the train across the country.

After they had been in their new home for a few days, Earl went into his mother's bedroom to talk with her. She still was suffering from the flu and was in bed.

"Earl," she said in a quavering voice, "I saw Mary many times before we left Bandon. She told me how she had been crushed by your letter calling off the engagement. In fact I didn't think she would recover from it. She was very distant for many weeks. Fortunately for her, she met another boy and I believe his name is John." Earl felt that old pang of jealousy stab him in the heart. Betty began coughing and couldn't seem to stop. Eventually the small dinner she had eaten came back up, too. Earl continued sitting on the bed close to his mother and held her as she shook with the chills. He held her for some time and after a while, she drifted off to sleep.

In his room Earl decided to write Mary a letter.

Dear Mary,

I'm sorry for not writing sooner, but many things have happened. First of all, I have called off my engagement to marry Sarah. This was done for many reasons, reasons I will explain to you when we meet again. My parents are here and have bought a house and I will live with them until I graduate. Mother is very sick with the flu and I fear for her life. She is asleep now as I write this letter, but she is very weak, barely able to keep food down. My father blames everything on me. He says since I called off our engagement, I have done nothing but make stupid decisions leading to chaos in our family. My father and I argue constantly and this makes mother weaker. My father and I have agreed to call a truce while mother lies in bed. So, though the arguing is abating I have the continuing threat of my mother's health.

My grades at college are suffering from all that is happening. The only bright spot in my life is my cousin Mark who is continually hounding me to forsake everything and take a wild adventurous sailing trip around South America. That of course is preposterous, because it is important that I stay here and care for my mother. I hope all is going well for you.

I am also writing in hopes you will forgive me. I have made a terrible mistake. I see that now and hope that it is not too late for us to get back together.

Love,

Earl

The letter was sent the next day. A few weeks later Earl received a reply from Mary.

Dear Earl,

Thank you for your recent letter. I'm always interested in what you are doing. I'm sorry to hear of your mother's illness, and hope that the situation between you and your father can be solved.

I'm in agreement with Mark's mother in regards to the dangerous trip around South America and I implore you not to do it.

In response to your asking me to forgive you, all I can say is that I am seeing John on a regular basis. I hope you know that of course, I forgive you. However, I'm undecided as to which way I will turn. I still love you and you know that; I will always love you. We have shared so much together that I simply can't ever forget you. But you really let me down. I just don't know if I could ever recover from another spell of depression like I suffered. But I know this: I simply can't return to the commitment we made before you left.

Love,

Mary

As Betty's condition worsened, Earl watched his father become more distant. Tom never let his wife see the hostility he harbored for his son, but whenever Earl and Tom were out of the house, the rage would boil over. Earl knew that his mother was aware of what was going on between them. The doctor had examined Betty again and told the family that her influenza had become pneumonia. A month after the Jacobs had set up residency in Cambridge, Betty died.

Earl knew what was coming. He suffered the loss of his mother and now the finely-honed hatred of his father. It finally was spoken out loud, "Why on earth did you commit such a terrible act of lust! Mary waited for you in Bandon. How could you do this thing? Because of these lustful acts toward your cousin, your mother is now dead."

In their last confrontation, Earl's father vowed he would never talk to Earl again. Earl moved out of his father's home and dropped out of Harvard. He focused his grief in his new found business: painting houses and hanging wallpaper. His business began to flourish and Mark asked him if he could help when he graduated from high school. When spring arrived the two cousins began working together. But, Earl longed to return to his hometown of Bandon. His cousin's desire for a sailing adventure around the Cape was becoming an appealing option. Maybe they could do both.

Chapter 15
Luther Crabb Escapes

As the Dairymen's League and Nestlé drifted towards contentious times, the small community of Bandon worked its way towards summer. The veil of the winter of 1922 slowly lifted, exposing the coastal town to more days filled with sunshine. John had work and a roof over his head, and he had Mary. She filled his life with a kind of happiness, hope and future he had never known. He imagined the time when he would ask Mary to be his wife. When one of those letters from Earl arrived, John was on tenterhooks, though. He was fearful that his wonderful life could be snatched away like his secure family life had been lost in a moment on the Columbia River Gorge.

All Mary had to do was mention a letter from Earl and his whole sense of safety would ebb away like a fast tide. John's hand instinctively would grab for his watch. He had learned that holding his watch helped control the terrible jealousy that raged in his soul. Even when Mary professed her love for John, he still feared losing it all. Hearing her assurance that she loved him could not take away that moment that John would see, that moment when Mary's eyes would light up when she told John about the latest letter from Earl. Mary would be graduating soon, and her graduation reminded John that this should have been his graduation as well, had the accident not happened.

John and Mary were seen on the streets of Bandon nearly every day after school. John would take a break from work and run to Bandon High. He would walk Mary to the stern-wheeler and they could talk. Sometimes it was a lazy talk about school, about work. Lately though, Mary was concerned about her parents decision to sign with the league.

One Saturday afternoon, John ran into Mary and her parents as they got off the boat. They were on their way to the Dairymen's League meeting. John walked with them although he wasn't certain it was right for him, a Nestlé employee, to be anywhere near a league meeting. They joined a river of people all walking toward the large community building. The door was flanked by league officials who greeted each farmer as they entered the building. Adam led the way to four empty chairs next to the aisle. John noticed that some of the more loyal league members gave him a cold stare: they knew where he worked. From somewhere behind him, John heard a low voice, "What's *he* doing here?" John turned as he felt a hand on his shoulder. "You a spy for Nestlé?"

"No. I've come with my friends," he said. He turned back around, and let his arm drape over Mary's shoulder. John didn't like the way the meeting progressed. The league leaders made Nestlé out to be the enemy of the farmers. John heard grumbling all around, and he knew that the league would get new members if Nestlé was the bad guy. John whispered to Mary, "Why do they insult Nestlé so much?"

Mary's father leaned across her lap to talk to John. "Without a big membership, we have no clout. We are honorable in our intentions but we need more representation from every small dairy farmer in order to control the price of milk."

"Adam, Nestlé has never given the farmers cause to distrust their business practices," John said. Just then a wad of paper bounced off John's head. He looked around and saw a few members laughing. John was irked but sat quietly as the speakers presented their case.

"All those in favor of the league raise your hands." Most of the crowd raised their hands including Mary's folks. "It is our purpose to represent you as a cooperative to the cheese, butter and canned milk manufacturers. In order to achieve the leverage we need to control the price of milk, we need everybody to join." Hoots and hollers went round the room.

The next speaker was Oregon State agriculturist, Mr. Pickle. "Ladies and Gentlemen, it is with great pleasure that I address you this afternoon. I would just like to start by saying that Mr. Teasdale here speaks the truth when he says you folks need to organize, join forces and stand up to the big corporations, especially the likes of Nestlé. It's the only way you will ever gain the power to control the prices for the product you work so hard to produce."

John couldn't believe his ears. How can they talk like this? This wasn't the Nestlé that he worked so hard for.

Mr. Pickle continued, "Consequently, you farmers have but two alternatives: you can go with the Dairymen's League, or you can go to *ruin*," he smacked the lectern with his fist, "by selling your milk directly to Nestlé." The last sentence was greeted with cheers and whistles. John felt like shouting back at the speaker but controlled himself. Another wad of paper hit John on the head. He turned, ready to go over his chair to find the perpetrator, but Mary's hand held him fast.

"Please, John, don't. You will only give them what

they want, and that's a big fight." She was right. Mary told him the meeting was almost over. The league president pleaded yet again to those farmers who weren't members to join. At the meeting's end, people filled the aisles walking out the door. John and the Bennett family walked out amid the crowd.

"John, I don't want you to come with us to league meeting again," Adam said, gravely.

"Father!" cried Mary. She looked at John and continued talking to her father. "John didn't do anything. Shame on you, Father!"

"Just the same, Mary, he caused a lot of unnecessary commotion. John did you hear me?"

"Yes, sir," John said.

On Monday John told his new superintendent, Wayne McLaughlin, about attending the league meeting. Wayne stood up suddenly from his chair and smashed his fist down on his desk.

"That Goddamn league! They insult our company! It's slanderous! We have invested thousands of dollars in this community. It's Nestlé who is building the new roads and the new water system. It's Nestlé who is building that new school. We're providing direct incentive programs to the dairy farmer. This Mr. Pickle should be dismissed from his state position because he's not at all impartial when talking about our company, and he should be. He's lucky we don't sue him. I'm going to write a letter to the state agriculture department and the Bandon newspaper. As John left the office, Wayne called to his secretary to come take a letter.

On Thursday evening, John read the *Western World* in his room. The superintendent's letter was featured prominently on the front page. John heard a knock on his bedroom door. John opened the door. "Did you see the paper?"

"Yes, Jake, I did. I hope all this league stuff doesn't ruin my relationship with Mary. Her father is already trying to discredit me in her eyes. I wish the league would just disappear. Some of these members are real radical ... no telling what they might do."

Jake said, "I think we are in for a battle, John. I'm really proud of our local newspaper editor. It took a lot of guts for Ben Harris to print our superintendent's letter. And I've heard rumors that some of the dairy farmers are planning to retaliate against Ben for this."

"That's ridiculous," John said. "Do you know which farmers?"

"No," Jake replied.

"Mary promised to go on a picnic with me after work on Friday, and it would be just my luck that her father's managed to talk her out of seeing me. It makes me tired," John blurted. Both men said goodnight and John crawled into bed with his worries.

Julia met both men at the foot of the stairs the following morning. "Did you hear?" she said. "The newspaper office was torched last night, and if it hadn't been for the local Coast Guard unit the whole town could have burnt down. Someone started the fire in the back of the building. Some local drunk who was sleeping behind some crab nets woke up and saw some men start the fire. He ran to the Coast Guard Station for help. The Guard men came running and put the fire out before it engulfed the whole building." John asked how she had learned all this. "I heard it just now from the milk man," Julia said.

"Jake, forget breakfast, let's leave right now and go look at the damage," John said.

The two men rushed out of the house towards

downtown Bandon. When they arrived at the newspaper building, Ben Harris was already there, assessing the damage. John saw that the whole back of the building was blackened, but it wasn't as bad as he had expected. There were still a lot of empty water buckets strewn around. The Coast Guard men had wheeled several big water kegs into the yard and had used hoses to douse the fire.

"Well," said Ben, "nothing was damaged on the inside, thanks to those brave men. I wish I knew who did this. I wouldn't put it past some vigilante group connected with the league. This fire won't stop my next issue, and believe me when I say I will print just who I think is responsible. This was a deliberate act of arson, an effort to suppress free speech. Acts of arson will not stop this newspaper from printing all sides to an argument!"

"Wow, great words, Ben. Anything we can do to help here?" asked John.

"No thanks, I got it under control; you boys go on to work," Ben responded. "Wait a minute, there's some other news you boys might be interested in. I heard yesterday that Luther Crabb broke out of prison. He killed two guards while escaping. It's rumored he's headed for our area. He's considered armed and very dangerous, so if you see him be sure to report it to the sheriff."

John couldn't believe it: Luther out of prison. Both he and Jake knew there would be trouble now. The two headed off toward Nestlé at a run, realizing they stood a chance of being late to work for the first time ever.

The heat of the Nestlé-league fight grew with the summer. Jane and Adam Bennett sent their milk off every day, as always, on the stern-wheeler towards Nestlé. Now that Mary had graduated, she came in on the boat on Fridays. She would spend the day helping Julia and her mother, and then spend the evening with John, Jake and Julia. The last Friday in August, the two couples had planned to share an evening meal of fried chicken and roasted corn-on-the-cob on the Bandon cliffs that overlooked the ocean, (the very spot that Mary and Earl called their secret hideaway) and watch the sunset by the light of a fire.

As the sun descended below the horizon it ignited the clouds in a fiery display brightly illuminating the clouds overhead. The food basket was filled with chicken bones and corncobs. Jake stoked the fire. In spite of the beauty of the night and the camaraderie of the two couples, the subject that would not go away was the local fight and the sides taken between the dairy owners and Nestlé. "Mary, I'm really worried about you and your folks. The league has filed an injunction against Nestlé, demanding that farmers who signed with the league and who still send their milk to the condensary, without league consent, not be paid."

"I knew this would happen," Mary said. "Nestlé refuses to buy milk from the league. My folks are going to lose money. It's not fair. I don't see how anyone is going to win now. I wish my folks would have listened to me."

"From what I understand, it's in the hands of the courts now, but it will take some time before they can figure this mess out," John said. "This isn't the only problem either. Did you hear that Luther Crabb escaped from prison?"

"My God, he will try and get us, I just know it! He's a very mean, vindictive person. I know he blames us for his jail time," Julia said, "I'm scared."

John pulled a gun out of his back pocket. "Jake and I have armed ourselves with pistols."

"I think Luther would like nothing better than to

kill us. We must be prepared. I feel much safer with this pistol stuck in my belt," said Jake.

John explained their plan for taking care of the families. John would spend nights at the Bennett farm while Jake would be at Julia's. "We don't know what Luther will do, but we have to assume he will try something."

Jake, trying to cheer up his friends, began wiggling his ears. "Jake, will you cut that out!" Julia said, smacking him and laughing at the same time. She had tried and tried, without success, to learn how to wiggle her ears. "Just how you do that is beyond me!" John tried, squinting his face one direction and then the other, but his ears stayed still. Mary couldn't get her ears to move either, although she could touch the tip of her nose with her tongue.

The sun had been down for hours and the fire was nearly spent. They picked up their blankets and basket then walked from the coastal cliffs back to Julia's house. John told Mary that he thought going home with her would be a smart move. While Mary waited with Julia in the kitchen, John threw his things into a satchel for spending a few nights at the Bennett's farm. He and Mary said their goodbyes and headed east toward the river. At the Brown's farm they took a dory and crossed the river to the Bennett's.

Chapter 16
Luther Returns

Foremost in Luther's mind were the two couples responsible for his imprisonment. Sometimes he could almost see that damned John Dowd.

Luther reasoned, "If I have to live as a wanted fugitive the rest of my life, then I will wreak havoc on John Dowd and his friends, and once I've taken care of Dowd I will take his precious watch as a souvenir." Even as the storm raged in his head, he kept his wits about him, enough so that he traveled two hundred miles undetected from the Oregon Penitentiary in Salem, down the Willamette Valley's rolling hills to Coos County.

It was late evening when Luther arrived in Coquille. He was on the west side of town, on the bank of the Coquille River, when he noticed a secluded farm house. Silently opening the yard gate, he stealthily crept towards the front door. He couldn't hear anything inside so he tried the door knob. It was open. He walked through and into the front room. Even in the dark he could see two doors off the front room; they were both closed. He tried the first one and it was a closet. Then he tried the other. As he carefully turned the knob, he heard a slight rustle on the other side. He continued to push the door open when all of a sudden he was blinded by a gun blast and a bullet grazed his temple.

Luther closed the door instantly and ran. Boom!!

Another bullet smashed through the door and tore a chunk of flesh from Luther's calf. He managed to get through the front door and outside. There was another shot behind him and Luther was relieved when no new pain hit him. Bleeding, he hobbled down to the boat dock. Fog had settled in and it clouded his vision. Luther climbed into a small fishing boat and began to row his way down the river towards Bandon.

John and Mary tied the Brown's rowboat to the Bennett dock and walked up the long gangway to the front door. Mary opened the door and called out to her parents, "John and I are here." She explained to her father about Luther's escape and the plan for John to stay with them in case Luther decided to try to harm the family. "We'll be out here on the front porch for awhile."

Jane came out of the kitchen and gave each of them a hug. "There's some leftover applesauce if you'd like."

"Not tonight, Mother. Why don't you two go on to bed, and John and I will lock up when we come in."

"Not much to see on the front porch with the thick fog out there," replied Mary's mother.

"We have some things to talk about and then we will be in, so go to bed and don't worry." There was a porch swing just to the left of the front door. While they talked, the swing creaked each time they pushed it back. After a time, their words gave way to kisses in the still night. Fog had enveloped the farm and John could see only about halfway down the gangway. Beyond the wall of fog was the flowing river.

Traveling with the current made rowing easy for Luther, almost like coasting. He spoke his thoughts into the fog, "Find the Bennett farm, kill Mary and her parents, and then hide out for a while. I'll get the others later." Luther was familiar with the hills behind Mary's place because he had logged in them for the Gainesville Saw Mill Company. As Luther inched his way along the fog-shrouded river, the currents pulled him past overhanging trees and through swirling eddies. In the fogged in pastures he could sometimes hear the lowing of a cow.

When Luther neared the Bennett farm he rowed the boat to the bank. He stepped onto the seat, lost his balance, and nearly dumped himself into the water. Once on the muddy shore he carefully replaced the oar in the boat and pushed the boat back out into the current. The boat drifted off and disappeared in the fog. Luther's feet sank in the mud as he slogged toward pasture and solid footing. He headed inland, passing calm cows chewing their cud, and then climbed over a fence toward the back porch of the Bennett house. A dog barked incessantly, and Luther waited for some dog to dash out of the fog and chew another chunk out of him. When no dog appeared, he relaxed some, knowing the dog was probably tied or maybe contained in some building.

At the first bark, John and Mary pulled away from each other, startled and alert. John took Mary's hand and led her around to the back of the house. Pup was straining at her collar and barking like a machine gun. The collie's eyes were riveted to the house. John had already drawn his pistol. As they both peeked around the corner, they saw Luther enter the back door of the house. "Oh my God! My parents!" John touched her lips to silence her.

"Does your father have a gun?" John whispered. Mary nodded, yes. "Stay here, I'm going into the house to try to stop this, once and for all." John ran up the back porch stairs and entered through the same door Luther had used. Just then, Luther came at John out of the darkness, a knife raised to strike. Although John was able to move out of the way, the knife still sliced into John's left shoulder and side. John swung around and got off one shot that must have hit Luther because he heard Luther's groan. John's shot didn't do enough damage though, as Luther was able to get out the back door, push his way past Mary, and disappear into the fog. He ran towards the forest covered hillside as the dog barked helplessly.

Adam Bennett came through the door with his shotgun raised to find John sitting on a chair holding his bloody left side. "He went that way. Be careful, Mary's still out there." Adam went through the back door and looked into the deep fog. Mary stood on the porch with her back to the house. Her hands were clenched over her mouth. Adam took her in his arms and then helped her back into the kitchen. John had managed to turn on a light. "There's no use trying to find that lunatic in this fog," said Adam. "We need to get you fixed up, young man." Mary grabbed some towels to stem the bleeding. Jane burst into the kitchen still in her nightgown, wide-eyed. She saw John bleeding and rushed to his side.

Adam retrieved some fishing line from his creel, then ordered Mary and Jane to boil water. Using one of Jane's sewing needles, Adam, with the deftness of a veterinarian, stitched John's skin back over the exposed flesh, while John downed half a bottle of moonshine to deaden the pain. Mary cradled John in her arms as he writhed in pain and clutched Mary for support.

Midway through the operation, there was a knock on the front door. When the door swung open, in walked Carl Brown from across the river. "I rowed over to see what all the commotion was," he said.

"Carl, go to town and get the sheriff and have him organize a posse: Luther Crabb took off for the mountains, after nearly killing John, here," Adam said. Carl was out the door in an instant, slamming it as he ran for his boat.

Blakely The Heirloom

Chapter 17

Since Luther knew the mountainous terrain, he knew where to hide. Stumbling through the salal, prickly shrubs, and towering Queen Anne's lace, he clumsily climbed up the hill. He remembered an old logging site that would be suitable to hide in, and there he could tend to his wounds. His big frame sliced through the hillside vegetation like a bear after honey. He found the clearing he sought and the old lean-to building, now hidden by young alder trees. Breathing hard, he leaned against the wall of the shed and rested like a wild animal that had just chased prey.

His exposed hands and face were cut and bleeding from the frantic escape through the underbrush. He examined his stomach wound. Actually the bullet had entered and exited his side. He figured there wasn't all that much damage, but it was still bleeding a little and felt like it was on fire. When he eased himself to the floor, his side ached like blue blazes. He knew he was lucky. He leaned back against the wooden wall and fell asleep.

He awoke a few hours later, and knew he must get moving, for he feared a posse would be looking for him. It was still dark, but dawn was teasing the eastern sky. His wounds ached as he plodded back down the mountain. At a dock just west of the Bennett's farm he found a small boat and rowed across the river. Once on the other side, he climbed the hill and walked and scrambled towards the woods that surrounded the Ferry Creek reservoir. This area was like home; he could hide out here until he could decide his next move.

It was morning when he reached the banks of the reservoir. The sun had risen above the mountains to the east. A steamy fog shrouded the reservoir like a cloud obscures a peak. On the uphill side of the lake he found a little cave and climbed in, settling down like a bear in hibernation. He slept, and when he awoke the sun was high overhead. His stomach wound ached. He heard a noise off in the distance that kept getting louder. As the sound grew, he was sure it was footsteps he heard. As he peeked out of his cave, he saw that he was exposed by the sunlight. The footsteps grew louder. Luther tried to move away from the light, but his body ached and all he could do was quietly hold his position. When he looked out again, he could make out the shape of a man, darkened by the sun that blazed behind him.

"Luther, is that you?" Luther recognized the voice at once: it was Matt.

Chapter 18
The Manhunt

At sunrise, Ben Harris was the first to arrive at the Bennett's farm.

"This is a major Oregon news story. I plan to accompany the posse and send my stories about how the chase is going to the Portland and Salem papers. I hope we can catch Luther."

It wasn't long after Ben arrived that the Bandon sheriff and his deputy, two state troopers and three posse members showed up. They all crowded into the front room, eager to set off because the day was sunny and conditions were good for the search. John sat on the couch and it was obvious to everyone he was still in a lot of pain. "I want to help," he said. He tried to stand, but he could not bear the pain. He fell back on the couch and Mary gasped and ran to his side, putting her arm around him. Soon, the posse headed out the Bennett's back door and started up the hill.

Later that evening around sunset, the bedraggled group returned to the Bennett farm, empty-handed. Ben read the article he had prepared for the big northern newspapers to John and Mary:

> In the search for Luther Crabb, the sheriff's posse came up empty-handed today. Yet there were some clues as to where Luther might have gone. As we climbed the mountains north of the Coquille River we followed foot tracks, and found blood spots along a trail that led to a

lean-to. We know that Luther had been in that building for a short time because of the blood. We followed his trail from the lean-to back down the hill to the river. The farmer at this location said someone had stolen his boat. We concluded that Luther could have gone west to Bandon, or east to Coquille. It is everyone's feeling that he went east. Tomorrow the search will continue.

Ben made every effort to keep John and the Bennetts up to date on how the search was evolving. Every time the stern-wheeler would go up river and make its stop at the Bennett's farm there would be a written letter from Ben. The last report stated:

We have been searching for a week without results. The posse has scoured Riverton, Coquille, and Bandon. This week, the Coos County Sheriff has decided to look in Coos Bay. The fact that there have been no sightings of Luther is puzzling. His mug shot is posted everywhere. If the posse has no success in Coos Bay, the search will be called off. There is always the possibility that Luther Crabb has died of his wounds in the mountains.

Chapter 19

While John recuperated from his wounds, he stayed at the Bennett farm. Nestlé had sent their wishes for his speedy recovery. In the mornings, he'd watch as Mary and her father would set the ten-gallon milk cans on the dock. From the front room window he could see the dock and he looked forward to when the stern-wheeler came and went. This particular morning he watched as Mary put out the milk cans and saw the big steamer approach. Mary waited to see if there was any mail. One of the crewmen handed her a letter.

Standing on the dock, she opened it. After reading the letter, Mary put it in her apron pocket and walked up the gangway to the front door. As she entered the living room. John said "Another letter from Ben?"

"No," Mary said.

"Who was it from?" John said.

"It's just a letter, nothing to be alarmed about," Mary said. She looked away.

"I'm not alarmed and I know who it's from," John's hand reached for his watch. "It's from Earl, isn't it?"

"Yes, it is," Mary said, "and I plan to write back."

John hated these letters, he hated how Mary still cared about Earl. He was afraid that his days with Mary were numbered. Mary ran into the kitchen hung up her apron and then told John she was going out to the barn to help her mother and father. After she left the house John noticed the apron and took the letter out and read it.

Dear Mary,

Since last I wrote, my mother has passed away. We had the funeral a week ago. I had to drop out of school. My father continues to blame me for my mother's death and I have moved out and am now on my own. My painting business is doing well, Mark is working in the business with me, and he is a very good worker.

Mark has not stopped hounding me to take a sailing trip around South America. I can't let him go on his own and if he ever decides to take the trip he'll need me to bring him home alive. Aunt Claudia insists that I go with him. If nothing else, the trip would be an exciting way to return to Bandon and to see you again. But for now I must concentrate my energies on my new work. I look forward to hearing from you.

I'm still very sorry for causing you such grief. I dream of getting back together.

Love,

Earl

John was just putting the letter back in Mary's apron when she returned to the kitchen. "Did you read my letter?" John heard anger in her voice.

John said, "Yes, and I'm already sorry. I don't know what made me do it."

"I'll tell you what made you do it. It's jealousy, plain old jealousy, and I'll not have you reading my personal mail! I'll tell you something else too. I've noticed that every time you think you are facing a dilemma you grab for your watch, as if that watch will solve whatever is bothering you. You should learn to face problems on your own and not rely on your good luck charm. That watch of yours is not what you think it is. You will have to learn to trust me, or I'll have nothing to do with you. When you have mastered these two problems then I will agree to see you again. Until then, I'll not even talk with you." Mary grabbed her apron and walked back outside toward the barn.

Chapter 20

The League Tries to Take the Bennett Farm

Mary was still not talking to John after three weeks of convalescence. John was now able to return to town and work at Nestlé. On his last morning on the Bennett farm, the sun rose over the tree tops and dissolved the fog, producing a beautiful morning. The blue Coquille River flowed amid green pastures in a fertile valley filled with well-fed, plump cows who waited to be milked, and milking was just the first of many other chores to be done every day. Mary had already done her morning milking chores. Adam had carried the full ten-gallon milk cans out to the dock and Jane had served them all breakfast of coffee, eggs, and rolls.

John walked down the Bennett gangway to the edge of the dock. The *John Wilde* was slowly approaching, water rippling on either side of the bow. As the cargo entry door loomed, deck hands jumped out onto the dock and loaded the Bennett milk cans. John jumped on the slowly moving vessel, and winced: his wounds still hurt. The Bennetts watched and Adam and Jane waved as the boat moved away from the dock. The big paddle wheel began to turn faster.

John ascended the stairs to the passenger deck and waved back to the Bennetts, but Mary didn't wave. Soon they disappeared in the distance as the stern-wheeler chugged down river towards Bandon. John felt as though he had lost Mary's love. He couldn't bear the thought of losing her. He yearned for her forgiveness, "Please Mary, talk to me again," he whispered. He had to do something, but right now he couldn't think of what to do. Instinctively, his fingers wrapped around his watch, hoping for some comfort and answers to his relations with Mary—the very thing that she had told him was the problem. What harm could touching his watch bring?

Turning, John found the second level crowded with dairymen.

One dairyman came up to John. "Were you aware that your employer has not paid us for our milk in over two weeks? We are going to town to see the Nestlé superintendent. He has promised to talk with us about the league situation. Some of the farmers are really mad. I hope a riot doesn't break out. All we want is our money."

"There he is," another farmer yelled and pointed at John. "He works for Nestlé. Why doesn't your company pay us for our milk? Why won't Nestlé buy league milk?" The farmer came nose-to-nose to John while making his accusations.

"Our company has never bought milk from the league. They have always maintained that policy, you know that," John responded.

Three more farmers joined in, accusing John as though he could change everything. They backed him up against the rail. Their arms where flailing as they yelled. It looked as though they were getting ready to throw John overboard.

"Wait a minute!" yelled one of the league leaders. "It's not John who is responsible for this mess, it's his company. We are supposed to find out today why they are not paying us. Remember, that's why we are on this boat. So leave John alone." The men backed off, leaving John by the rail.

John straightened his clothing and walked to the front of the passenger section. He watched as the boat wended its way down river towards Bandon.

John helped serve coffee to the dairymen as they waited in the crowded Nestlé cafeteria for the superintendent to address them. When the superintendent came into the room, he stepped up on the platform. "It's not my intention to bore you with unnecessary facts; it will not take long to explain why you are not getting the money you so rightfully deserve. The Dairyman's League has filed an injunction against Nestlé. What the league is saying is that those of you who belong to the league have broken your contractual agreement by selling your milk directly to us. As you know, we will not buy milk from the league, resulting in this injunction. The state courts are in the process of making a ruling. Until that ruling is made, Nestlé is restricted from paying you your money. I hope this explains to you the dire predicament we are facing. Are there any questions?" The superintendent pointed to a man in the front row, who stood and faced the superintendent.

"Why don't you buy milk from the league?"

"It's been our long-standing policy to never buy from a league or union, not here in Bandon, not anywhere else either. We are fair and honest in our dealings with the dairy farmer and resent the Dairymen's League saying we cheat farmers."

Another man stood. "We are not calling you unfair, we just want our money. We want Nestlé to take another look at buying milk from the league. Why can't you at least try it? It's pure idiocy to maintain a rigid policy that's clearly not working." Hoots and shouts went up around the room. The farmers were standing and they were mad. John could hardly blame the dairymen for their harsh attitude towards Nestlé. He didn't think the superintendent's answers had been at all adequate.

The Superintendent said, "That's all I have to say on the subject for now. We will try to keep you informed of any major decisions, but until that time, please be sensible in your dealings with us. Thank you and good afternoon." The superintendent quickly left the room.

It was 8 p.m. and John was seated at the kitchen table sipping coffee at the boarding house. Julia walked in and sat down. "I saw Mary in town today. She says she wants to see you again. She's sorry about how harsh she was on you."

"She was right. I meddled in her affairs with Earl," John said.

"She says to tell you she will be in town tomorrow, and if you wouldn't mind, she would like to spend the night here."

"Of course, I don't mind! My every waking hour I think about her, and how she is doing," John said, "Please tell her to come. Or better yet, I'll meet her at the stern-wheeler myself in the afternoon." He felt his watch and couldn't stop the thought that it had brought about a miracle. John slept the night through for the first time in weeks.

Canned milk production was down at the condensary because farmers were refusing to bring Nestlé any milk. Instead, they were selling their milk to the cheese companies. Cheese was a growing business for the dairymen. The Nestlé company started closing early and laying off workers. These conditions allowed John to get off work in time to meet Mary at the boat. He was nervous, waiting as the boat eased close to the dock. Mary didn't wave, but she did smile. She reached for John's hand, and they walked hand-in-hand to the beach and found a place to sit in the sand. They cuddled close as the sun hung over head.

"Mary, these last few weeks I have realized that I can't live without you. I dream constantly of us being together and starting a family. Would you be my wife?" John said.

Mary's head rested on John's chest and she looked up into John's eyes. Stretching, she kissed him on the lips saying softly, "I can't, not yet. I hope you will forgive me about the letter," Mary said. "You apologized at the time and I was so fuming mad I didn't take you at your word. Besides, if we were to marry we must learn to share everything. We can't have any secrets."

"Mary, I'm as much to blame as you are, but that's now in the past, we must now look towards the future."

"I dearly want to live with you, but I'm just uncertain as to what to do. There are so many things happening right now. Earl is about to risk his life on a wild sailing adventure, and the league has filed suit against my family for selling milk to Nestlé. Since we don't have much money, the league could take our farm. Everything is a mess!"

Chapter 21

After their reunion, Luther and Matt set up camp near the Ferry Creek reservoir. Luther's wounds were still sore, yet they were healing. Matt was still hampered by having only one good arm. Adjacent to their campsite was Burt's still operation. Burt invited the two newcomers over to taste his latest batch of whiskey. They all sat on rough-hewn seats made from stumps. Ferry Creek drifted lazily past them and alders lined the bank. Towering cedars claimed the evening sky. Burt's small cabin was barely visible in the declining light. The three men downed enough whiskey to float a stern-wheeler.

"When I was in town today I was approached by two league members who hate Nestlé. They know where I make my brew and asked me if I would blow up the water flume that carries water from the reservoir to the Nestlé plant. They said they would pay me well if I would do their bidding."

"What did you tell them?" Luther asked.

"I told 'em no," said Burt gruffly. "Hey, what do you think of my whiskey? I just drew it from the keg today. Here, try some from this jug." Luther grabbed the jug and took a big swig and then he handed it to Matt. Matt took a big gulp too, like Luther's, and as the jug fell to his lap he let out a big hot gasp. "Wow," he hooted, "that almost took my head off!"

"Very potent, and not bad," Luther slurred. "How could Matt and I contact these Nestlé-hating men?"

"Their names are Frank and River and you can find them at the Oriental Building. They hang out at the speakeasy located at the back near the stairs that lead up to the brothel. Tell 'em I sent you." Luther and Matt took a few more swigs from the jug and then decided to return to their camp.

"Thanks for the information and moonshine. Maybe we'll see you in the morning," Luther said. The two conspirators walked back to their camp. As they lay under their covers, their fire crackled between them. Looking up through the tree limbs Luther could see an evening sky filled with stars. "Tomorrow morning we'll figure out what we're gonna do," Luther said. "Right, boss," Matt croaked. "Glad you're back." They both fell asleep.

The next morning Luther smelled coffee brewing when he awoke. Matt was sitting next to the fire. Luther got up slowly and put on his boots. The coffee had finished perking by the time Luther sat down next to Matt. With his good arm Matt poured him a cup of coffee. After pondering the current situation, Luther said, "My father taught me how to make whiskey when I was sixteen. I still remember how to do it. Burt has plenty of ingredients to get us started making our own brew. We could make lots of money if we were to take over his operation." Matt's eyes sparkled at the thought. "Plus we can make money blowing up that flume. Listen, you go into town and find these guys Frank and River; tell them we'll do their nasty job. While you're gone I'll take care of Burt." Matt finished his coffee, put on his hat and quietly left camp.

Luther drank two more cups of coffee and poured a third. He could see Burt working at his still. He was carrying big sacks of sugar from his cabin over to a barrel. Luther pulled out his knife and tested its sharpness against his finger. His coffee had gotten cold so he threw it out and it splattered on the ground. He stuck the knife back in his scabbard and walked in Burt's direction, as he busily threw whiskey-making ingredients into the barrel. He wasn't the neatest fellow, Luther noticed, because there were empty sacks strewn on the ground. Luther noiselessly approached. Burt was engrossed in his work, lifting a sack of sugar up to the rim of the barrel to rest it on the edge. Luther watched him slit the top of the sugar sack and as he finished his cut, Luther drew his knife edge horizontally across Burt's throat. The bag of sugar slid back to the ground, spilling little. Luther lowered the quivering body to the ground and dragged it out of camp. He dug a shallow grave and buried Burt.

Luther went back to his camp and picked up Matt's and his belongings and moved them to the small cabin next to the still. Finally he went about completing the operation of putting the sugar in the barrel. He and Matt now had a means of making a living.

Soon, he would do to John and his friends what he had done to Burt. For the time being, he must be careful because he knew there were "Wanted" posters up all over town. For now he must remain out of sight. He knew Matt's face was not as familiar and he would have to rely on him to get supplies and sell their new found bonanza.

Later that day Matt came back with some explosives and a fistful of cash. "We'll get another payment as soon as we blow up the flume," Matt said.

"We'll get to work on it right now," Luther replied.

They walked to the downhill side of the reservoir and followed the flume for a way, slashing their way through the thick brush. They came to a level spot. Luther ordered Matt to put the explosives on the wood bracing that held the flume above the shrubbery, and then they stretched a long fuse up the mountain. Luther lit the fuse and they both scrambled up the hill. BOOM!!! It wasn't a big break but big enough to divert the water from the flume into the forest. Matt smiled, wrinkling the skin around his beady eyes. On their way back to camp Luther told Matt about the still operator and their new business.

Chapter 22

Jake and John pushed through the squeaky door and headed off to work. John was quiet as they walked. He worried about Mary's folks: where would they get the money to pay the league if the league won their lawsuit? Why doesn't Mary accept his proposal of marriage? Does she still love Earl? Mary gave no reason that she did, yet all these letters... However, Mary had made it clear to John she was strongly committed to him. Not only that, they had spent many nights together in intimate love. John was still unsure what she would decide. These thoughts washed through his mind as he and Jake arrived at Nestlé.

It was late in the afternoon when they were notified of the water problem. Water was not coming down the flume and the company needed this water source to make their canned milk. They had a water tank and could finish out the day's operations, but someone was going to have to check why the water had dried up. The superintendent sent some carpenters out to see if there was a break in the flume, and repair it if that was the problem. John and Jake were let off work early.

On their way back to the boarding house Jake said, "I'm starting to worry about our jobs. Julia and I were counting on my working here should we get married. We're let off early more and more."

"I know what you mean, I'm worried too. The farmers don't want to send us their milk, and now this water problem," John said.

"I'm sure it's league fanatics responsible for this flume damage, or whatever is making the water stop flowing," Jake reasoned. John agreed.

The next day John was called to the superintendent's office.

"John, I want you to be aware that Nestlé is taking a serious look at its Bandon plant. If our problems here persist, then it looks like we will have to close down. The flume will take a few more days to repair, but the milk intake is still way down."

John said, "Has the court come to a decision on the contracts yet?"

"I just received this envelope on that subject. Let me read it." And the superintendent opened the letter that was on his desk. His expression changed immediately. "We've won the court case!! The courts have ruled that the league contract unduly restrains trade. In effect, what that means is the farmers can now be paid, and all the farmers, whether league members or not, can send their milk here."

John asked, "Do you know how that will affect the case of the Dairymen's League vs. Bennett?"

"This individual suit against your friends is the last avenue the league has to legally make their contracts enforceable. They will fight this case to the bitter end. Plus, there are other troublemakers out there who will stop at nothing to close our plant down. This latest verdict will incense them."

"How does this new information affect our plant?" John asked.

"Why, it's the best news we could have received. I suspect the intake of milk will now increase to record levels. The only impediment to this would be if your friends lost their suit. Nestlé will be glad to provide money and legal counsel for them," the superintendent said.

"I will pass that information along to the Bennetts, and I'm sure they will gladly accept any financial help you can provide. Thank you," John said.

On their way home from work, John explained the latest good news to Jake.

"Julia will be glad to hear this, too. If Nestlé closed, her mother would lose boarders. She'd never make it," Jake said.

"There are still some league men who will see this as a direct slap in the face. I hope they can just accept it and let it pass and not retaliate against Nestlé," John said.

Chapter 23

John arrived at the Bennett house early in the evening. The Bennett family settled in the front room with John and Mary sitting across from the older couple. John told the Bennetts of the proposal of financial and legal help from Nestlé.

"All we can do now is wait," Adam said. "In the meantime, we'll carry on with the milk business as usual."

John and Mary moved out onto the front porch. They sat on the swing as the river flowed lazily by. It was a clear evening and they watched as the mountains formed a jagged line in the horizon.

"I have to share something with you," Mary said. John's fingertips instinctively touched the cool metal of his watch. "Today I received a letter from Earl. He writes that he is going to take this foolish sailing trip around the Cape. I feel certain that this is his cousin's idea. Mark has been hounding Earl for a long time and his mother pleads with Earl to go with him. I think Earl is using this trip as an escape from his misfortunes. Earl has suffered his mother's death, his father's estrangement, flunking out of college and now business failure. He's probably not thinking clearly," and as tears swept down her cheeks she said, "I fear for his life." John wrapped his arms around Mary and drew her close. Later, they went inside to their separate beds.

Chapter 24

As the two men stood on the docks of New York's harbor they looked out to sea. Earl smelled the salt air and watched as seagulls circled overhead. One gull perched on top of a mast. In the distance was a huge sailing vessel with all of its sails unfurled. As it neared the harbor the sails were slowly furled. Mark, who was four inches taller than his red-haired cousin, looked down on him and raved. "That's our ship, Earl. It's a windjammer! All my life I've dreamed of sailing on one of those." Earl looked and it was indeed a beautiful sight. There were other ships in the harbor too: steamers, launches, tug boats, fishing boats, and a few huge windjammers. The four or five windjammers looked like skeletons as they reposed at the docks with their sails furled.

Earl listened as his excited cousin talked about the big ships. "There, look," Mark said. "That's the *PJ Thomas*, a three-master, and there's another, the *Gustina*. Earl couldn't believe how stirred up his cousin was. "Look Earl, a four-master ship, the *Blakely*. "That's the good ship *Mishuli* with a foremast at the bow, mainmast, mizzenmast, and jiggermast at the stern. That top sail on the fore mast is called the Royal." Mark's excitement was beginning to infect Earl. He fantasized being captain on a windjammer out on the open seas with sails unfurled, the wind pushing the ship forward, water splashing off the bow and clouds threatening on the horizon. "Sail on lads, sail on! Bandon and Mary, here I come!"

When Earl came out of his trance they were standing by the *Padal*. He looked up at the rail of the ship and there was a young man looking down at him. He watched as the man walked down the gangway, his blond hair flopping against his brow. He looked to be the same age as Mark and Earl. "We sail tomorrow, care to come along?" the man jokingly asked. Earl responded without hesitation, "Aye, aye Sir," and laughed as he said it. Mark mimicked him and both saluted their new young friend.

"Let me introduce myself. My name is Doug Gilbertson and this is my ship. My grandfather, a former ship builder in Coos Bay, Oregon, commissioned me to buy a ship, a full rigged steel ship, this windjammer, and sail it around Cape Horn to Coos Bay. The *Padal* is a four-masted vessel with a running rigging. She has a raised mid-ship and she is twenty-three years old." He then went on to explain every facet of his new purchase.

"This ship is 300 feet long, 44 feet wide and 24 feet deep. She weighs 2,450 tons, and was originally designed for cargo but later was turned into a training ship. This is a rare find, because she has been maintained in her original condition and not used extensively in hauling ventures. It is a great treasure bought on the declining market of sailing windjammers; their use is slowly being extinguished."

Earl said, "Let me see if I understand you correctly. You're from Coos Bay and you are to sail this treasure back to Coos Bay tomorrow?"

"We leave at 6 a.m.," Doug said.

Earl and Mark gasped; they just couldn't believe their good fortune.

"Grandfather wanted me to buy a true steel-hulled windjammer, European made, and then possibly use the ship for the West Coast lumber trade or maybe

make a museum out of it, or possibly sell the ship at
a profit on the West Coast. Any one of these plans
could happen. I bought the ship in Wilmington, North
Carolina. I just sailed into port here two days ago. Two
of our crew deserted this morning and we need two
more men. Would you two be willing to come aboard
as sailors? The work is hard and dangerous, and many
have perished sailing around the Horn, the food is
awful, the pay is low and we will be at sea for three to
four months, maybe longer. What do you say?"

Earl had but one question: "Are you qualified to
sail such a ship?"

"I have been on sea going vessels since I was
a child. My grandfather has taught me a lot and I
have captained many ships up and down the West
Coast with cargos of lumber. But," he said, "I have
never sailed around the Horn. My grandfather says
that in order to become a true sailor, a 'shellback' he
calls them, I must sail around the Horn. Once I have
accomplished this feat, he told me I would be able
to confront any sailing situation on the West coast.
So, why not come with me on this adventure of a
lifetime?"

Earl had no choice; he knew his cousin's feelings,
and he wouldn't let his cousin go by himself. Earl
also wanted to take his mind off his past misfortunes.
Another powerful force influencing his decision was
the fact that Mary was still undecided about her future.
Earl signed first, and Mark signed next. They were on
their way around Cape Horn on the windjammer *Padal*.

Chapter 25

Luther worked the still operation with enthusiasm. Both he and Matt were making good money from their new-found, but illegal, profession. It took Luther a while to remember the whole process of making whiskey, but with the aid of Burt's equipment and the system that he had laid out, it wasn't long until he kept liquor flowing at an even pace. It seemed that the demand for the product was greater than he was able to manufacture. Using Burt's donkey, Matt would carry heavy loads of whiskey to town and then return with needed supplies. One morning, Matt took the donkey loaded down with jugs into town to sell to local vendors. While in town he bought supplies of yeast and grain, with more yeast than usual. Later that day Luther was busy capping jugs when Matt sauntered into camp.

"Frank and River have come up with another plan to destroy the Nestlé Company. They have another cash offer for us," Matt said.

"Do they want us to blow up the flume again?" Luther asked.

"No, they want us to pollute the water that goes to Nestlé," Matt said.

"Just how do they propose we do that?" Luther blurted.

"They want us to throw our refuse and large quantities of yeast into their water supply," Matt replied. "They gave me money to buy the yeast and said that we should be as close as possible to the plant when throwing it in the water."

"I wonder why they want us to throw yeast in the water? How will that pollute the water? I can understand our refuse because it might also plug up Nestlé's machinery. Where are Frank and River getting all this money to pay us?" Luther asked. Matt said he didn't know. "Oh well, who cares as long as they are paying us. When Nestlé goes out of business, then our enemies, John and Jake, will be out of a job. I like the way things are turning out."

Luther finished capping off the jugs. "This will be our first attempt at ruining the water, so help me carry this barrel of refuse to the flume and we'll dump it in." After they had accomplished that task, Luther said, "Now let's load up the donkey with some bags of yeast and take it down closer to the plant. We just have enough time before dark to dump the stuff in the water. Say, when do we get paid for this job?" Luther asked. "My next visit to town," Matt said.

Chapter 26

Earl and Mark were given oil skins (rain clothing and rain hats), and were assigned cots in the crewmen's quarters. Next they were introduced to the crew. A few of the men had been ashore during the day and night; some were carried back on board because they were too drunk to walk. The rest were a rag-tag group of sailors, wharf rats, and adventurers. Earl counted twenty-two crew members including the two first officers. Most of the crew was young, maybe twenty-one or so. Captain Gilbertson introduced Earl and Mark to the first officers. Frank Helmuth was in charge of the forward end of the ship and the foremast sails. The other officer was Sam Knudsen, and he was in charge of the mainmast and the mizzenmast plus other rear sails.

Gilbertson said to Earl, "The first officers are seasoned salts with leadership skills in running a windjammer. They're responsible for your training." Helmuth chose Earl to work the foremast, and Knudsen spoke for Mark for the mainsail and mizzenmasts.

That afternoon, Gilbertson accompanied Earl and Mark on a shopping trip into town to purchase the warm clothes they would need for the journey. "You'll also need a straight-edged knife and scabbard. A knife is a handy tool, so keep it on your belt at all times," Gilbertson told them.

Next morning, the crew hoisted and stowed the anchor. The *Padal* was ready to sail: full water tanks, hatches battened down, loose gear cleared from the decks and stowed, the gear wheel well-oiled, and lifeboats lashed in place. As a tug pulled the *Padal* out to sea, Earl felt the decks sway on the tide. A gentle breeze pressed against his skin and the smell of salt air filled his nostrils. Earl watched as the tug unleashed the windjammer and he grasped the rail as a helpless feeling rose in his belly. The *Padal* caught the tide and eased out to sea.

Frank Helmuth took Earl up the shrouds and showed him how to unfurl the sails. While hanging to the webbing, Frank yelled, "We're headed due east so that we can catch the southern winds that will take us south to South America and Cape Horn."

Earl and Mark were learning what was required of seamen. It was good that both men were in excellent condition. Earl was finding out that they would need every ounce of strength and endurance they could muster. The next couple of weeks were jammed with learning ship terminology, unfurling and furling the sails, and climbing the shrouds that led to the top most yardarms. Earl, one hand hanging on for dear life to the yards, had to work his other arm and hand at maneuvering the massive canvas sails and furling them in place. He did all this while he was standing on a rope a hundred feet in the air, trying desperately to maintain his balance as the large masts would tilt from side to side in the rolling sea. One thing that Earl quickly understood was that a fear of heights and a lack of agility meant the sailor's life was not for you. From a top vantage point on the yardarm, Earl was amazed at how small the crew on the deck looked; from the top of the yardarm, the *Padal* looked like a toy.

Captain Gilbertson invited Earl and Mark to his cabin for an evening meal. Earl was awed at how luxuriously the room was furnished. In the center was a large table, and hanging over it was a beautiful chandelier. As the chandelier swayed from side to side he noticed a wood stove, a huge roll top desk, plush rattan chairs, and walls finished in intricately carved mahogany wainscoting. The table had been set for four; Earl and Mark stood, waiting for some sign from the Captain to be seated. "Well, men, I am pleased with how well you two are doing. Both my first officers have let me know that you are both enthusiastic, hard working, fast learners. This is a difficult and dangerous trade, and you are doing a fine job." Gilbertson motioned for Earl and Mark to sit, and just then Earl saw an old man coming through the cabin door. Earl watched the old man make his way to the empty chair. "Let me introduce my friend. This is Captain Eric Hansen." Hansen had a mass of stark white hair that covered his head and chin and it hung down to his shiny belt buckle. He was thin and bent with age yet still a full six feet tall, and he moved with agility. Earl thought Hansen might be seventy or so. Hansen's gray eyes sparkled as he nodded to the young men.

"On at least thirty occasions Captain Hansen has directed steel barques around Cape Horn. He's a good friend of my grandfather and he advised me on the purchase of this ship, plus he's here to help guide us around the Horn. My grandfather said Captain Hansen had to go with me as my guide before he would let me make this voyage. Hansen has the power to override any order that I utter. Should anything happen to me he will be in full command." The four men ate the sumptuous meal quietly, yet Earl sensed concern about the upcoming journey. After dinner, Earl and Mark said goodbye and left for the starkness of their bunks.

The sleeping area always had a few men who were

not on a shift. Candles flickered as Earl and Mark entered the cramped room. Earl heard concern here as well. The sailors were recounting their previous hardships of the Horn. Earl and Mark crawled into their bunks and listened.

"On my last voyage we lost three men in the icy cold near the tip of South America. They were washed overboard all at the same time by one huge wave," said one. Another crewman said, "In my last voyage we had a man fall from the mast; he landed on the deck and died shortly afterward. He'd lost his grip and slipped on the icy rigging."

Mark whispered to Earl, "What have I got us into, I never dreamt it would be this dangerous." Earl whispered back, "It'll be all right, as long as we watch out for each other. As the captain said, we are in for the adventure of our lives. I feel a lot safer after meeting with Captain Hansen. I think Doug knows his business, but the old man makes me more confident with his vast experience. He will guide us through the hazardous stretches of this trip."

"I'm getting sick," whispered Mark. "God, I wish this boat would quit rocking." Mark jumped from his cot and ran out the door. Earl heard him come in later and he looked deathly ill. It wasn't long before Mark rushed out the door again. Mark never really got to sleep before he had to dash out, and then it was 2 a.m. and both men had to take their work shifts.

They climbed out on deck. Overhead Earl witnessed a dark sky afire with billions of stars the likes of which he had never witnessed before. They finished out their shift and then took their naps again. Mark finally slept. By their next shift it was day.

Helmuth informed Earl, "We are sailing at about

ten knots with favorable wind." Earl noticed a large steamer approaching their aft on the starboard side. The steamer came abreast the windjammer and the two ships stayed even for about a nautical mile. Then the steamer ratcheted up its power, and smoke belched from its stacks. The steamer moved right on past the four-masted barque. The steamer's passengers lined the deck pointing and laughing as they steamed by.

Captain Gilbertson came over to Earl and said, "Windjammers are a product of the past, a relic that has had better days. Windjammers used to carry large cargos of grain, nitrates, coal, guano, and copper; now steamers like that one are slowly taking over that trade." Earl's experience thus far had been so positive that he lamented the fact that these great ships were losing the battle as cargo carriers. Then a strange thing happened. Earl saw Captain Hansen come on deck. The old captain was watching the steamer chugging past the *Padal*.

"First officers Helmuth and Knudsen, stand by for orders. Unfurl the topsails," he shouted in a loud commanding voice. The crew climbed the shrouds with alacrity. Earl climbed the foremast followed by three other lads, and he watched as Mark climbed the mainmast followed by three men. Other crewmen climbed the mizzenmast. Even on his high perch Earl could hear Captain Hansen ordering the helmsman, "Steady as she goes." He shouted specific orders to the two first officers who responded like machines. The big top sails slowly opened up and grabbed the full force of the winds. The large windjammer increased its speed. Slowly the majestic windjammer caught up with the steam ship. The two massive hulks were neck and neck again.

Earl listened as the old captain continued issuing orders aft, stern, port, starboard and aloft. The clear calm orders came in rapid succession. He pushed the helmsman from the wheel, "Take charge of the aft sail, officers have all the sails unfurled, brace the yards!" Looking to the fore of the ship he barked, "Cook, stand by the foresheet." The crew was responding as if in a magical spell. "Helmsman, come back and steer." The crew had the windjammer flying, every rectangular sail puffed out and straining against the great steel masts. The masts leaned forward and the *Padal* quietly surged ahead of the steamer. The steamer's crew tried to increase the mechanical power, but there was no more power to be had, and on this windy day the steamer was left in the wake of the historic windjammer.

As the *Padal* sailed ahead Earl could see the steamer passengers who were now sober-faced, in contrast to the enthusiasm of the *Padal* crew. They laughed, shook hands, and rejoiced in their victory. Earl watched below and saw Captain Eric Hansen return to the captain's quarters. Gilbertson resumed command, a satisfied look on his young face. Earl lowered himself to the deck and Mark came over to his position.

"This is what I have dreamed of doing my whole life!" Mark shouted above the wind and ship's noise. "Finally at long last I am experiencing it!"

Earl couldn't help feeling the excitement of the moment, but he dreamed of something else: he dreamed of Bandon and that Mary just might wait for him.

Chapter 27

On Friday, John left work early and raced to the docks to meet Mary. He knew that Earl's last letter before his voyage had profoundly affected her and he feared Mary's affection for Earl. Might Mary think more of Earl for braving the sea than of him, as someone who worked in a condensary? He thought their closeness had changed again, and he didn't like that at all. Then he saw her coming down the gangway in a beautiful full length colorful gingham dress the color of the summer sky. The dress clung to her body like a glove and revealed her alluring femininity. John's insides felt like jelly, just like the first day he had met her. His hand went to his pocket and his heirloom as he proceeded up the gangway, meeting her halfway.

"I have some good news," John said. "The league has lost the case against your parents. They do not have to worry about losing their farm."

"That's great news, John. I can hardly wait to tell Father," Mary said. "Thank you for all your help."

"With all this league stuff behind us, Nestlé should expand, making this factory once again the biggest in the United States," John said.

Hand in hand, they entered the boarding house through the squeaky front door. "I'd put a drop of oil on those hinges, but Mrs. Smith tells me not to because it lets her know someone is either coming in or going out." Jake and Julia were sipping coffee and smiling.

"Are you hiding something from us," Mary said.

"Maybe," Julia said.

"Come on, quit teasing us. Tell us what is happening," John said.

Julia uncovered the top of her left hand and there, encircling her finger, was an engagement ring.

"I have proposed to Julia and she has accepted my offer. With Nestlé doing well now, we felt that it was the time for us to marry," Jake said. "We plan to elope to Roseburg next weekend. After that we will live here until we can afford a place of our own," Julia said. John wasn't surprised with the revelation. He sipped his coffee and thought he could hardly wait to make the same proposition to Mary. Julia and Jake left for a walk.

"Mary."

"I think I know what you're going to ask me," Mary said, "but right now I just can't. My folks are getting older and it's harder and harder for them to run the dairy. They need me there." They both finished their coffee and didn't say any more. Jake and Julia came in laughing and giggling through the front door.

In the middle of the night, Mary touched John on the cheek and said, "You must trust me." Several more silent minutes passed, and just after the clock struck three, John snuck back to his own room.

Back in his bed, John thought about Mary and couldn't help thinking that maybe she was waiting for Earl. "Why can't she say yes to me, especially since Nestlé's future looks so bright and the Dairymen's League threat is over?" John wondered. In this state of confusion, he fell asleep.

Ben Harris wrote his obituary of the league like this:

The Dairymen League Succumbs

The league tried to represent the farmers as best they could.

Even now at this late date, league administrators still feel they can represent the farmer better as a group than the farmer can represent himself alone. League administrators said they worked hard for this to happen. Even at last weeks' league meeting, its members were still trying to ward off being dissolved. The president tried everything he could to coax the league's members into staying with the foundering association. By the end of the meeting it was evident that the Dairymen's League was finished. It is my opinion had the league been more flexible in its contractual agreements, and had they emphasized that they would sell the farmers milk to only the cheese and butter concerns, then they may have survived the contentious atmosphere that erupted and resulted in their demise.

Chapter 28
The Marriage

With the league out of the way, Nestlé entered into a new era of prosperity. Nestlé continually provided optimistic reports to the Bandon newspaper of how well the business was doing. New dairy routes were opened up, and all dairy farmers to the east and down the coast were encouraged to send their milk to the Bandon Plant. New markets for condensed milk opened up overseas and at home. The Nestlé plant was the model condensary for the United States and the world.

John was in his room one evening reading the paper. The last rays of sunlight poured over his shoulder as he read. The Bandon newspaper reported some strange and unexplained incidents. Two loggers had been shot in the back while walking to work, and their bodies had been found right on the logging trail. John knew of other unexplained shootings around town. He and Jake had been shot at as they had walked to work just a few weeks ago, and whoever was doing these fiendish acts eluded the sheriff. John wondered if Luther was alive. He knew he'd shot him in the stomach, and that he could have died in the woods, but he wasn't certain. According to the article on the most recent shootings, "The sheriff is following up on every clue."

John folded his paper and looked out the window. He thought about Earl sailing on the open seas. What an adventure that would be; he envied Earl that. John wondered what would happen to his relationship with Mary when Earl returned home, as he was certain to do, and soon. John checked his watch and went to bed. It took some time before he could stop thinking about Earl and go to sleep.

When John met Mary at the boat on Friday afternoon after work, he noticed that she seemed happy and sad at the same time. At least that was the way John interpreted it. As they walked towards the boarding house, Mary slipped and would have fallen had it not been for John's quick reflexes when he caught her.

"John, I have something to tell you, and this is as good a time as any," Mary said as she regained her stance. "I've been experiencing morning sickness and I really think I'm pregnant. My mother told me we should marry as soon as possible." John could hardly believe his ears.

"This is the best news I have ever heard!" John smiled broadly and grabbed Mary in his arms and lifted her high in the air. "Careful John, you'll drop me! Careful!" Mary said. "I'll tell my folks when I get back home that we plan to wed. Mother said that they would handle all the marriage preparations." The sun was setting in the sky as they walked, but for John the day was just dawning.

The next week John was in the Superintendent's office again. Wayne McLaughlin looked up from his desk. "Wayne, Mary Bennett and I are engaged to be married. Could I count on you being an usher at my wedding?"

"My wife and I would be delighted to attend, and I consider it an honor to be asked," the superintendent said.

John said, "Jake is my best man and Julia's the bridesmaid. The wedding will take place in the Methodist church. We are expecting about 200 people. Mary Tyler has accepted our invitation to play the organ and sing. Pastor MacDonald will officiate. Mary's parents, oh gosh, my in-laws! My in-laws are arranging all of this wedding rigmarole!"

Ben Harris put the proceedings on the front page of the Bandon newspaper.

Basketball Hero to Marry

Mary Bennett has accepted a proposal to marry John Dowd. The two will be married this coming Sunday at the Methodist church, and Pastor MacDonald will preside. The festive proceedings are scheduled to begin at 2 p.m. Everyone in town is cordially invited to come. After the ceremony there will be a reception at Mrs. Smith's boarding house on Ocean Avenue. We are all looking forward to the union of these two fine Bandon citizens.

Sunday finally arrived. At 1:55 p.m., John was looking nervously at his treasured pocket watch as he hurried up the aisle to the waiting pastor and Jake. He returned the watch to his pocket and assumed his position next to Jake. Everyone looked toward the back of the sanctuary and waited for the organist to signal the arrival of the bridal party, and it didn't take more than a moment. John let his eyes rest for about two seconds on Julia in her lovely pale blue gown and then it was the breathtaking beauty of Mary, in full wedding attire, that filled his vision. She appeared with her father at the sanctuary's entrance.

At the first chord of the wedding march from Mrs.

Tyler's fingers, the entire assembly rose as one and Mary began her measured walk down the aisle, led by the enchanting three-year-old Monica, Mrs. Tyler's daughter. Monica tossed rose petals on the carpet and grinned from ear to ear. Mary and her father walked very slowly, giving Monica plenty of time to do her flower girl duties. Ben, from the *Western World*, snapped so many flash pictures that John thought he would see blue spots before his eyes for the rest of his life. When he could see again, it looked like Monica had stopped walking and was rubbing her eyes. She dropped her basket of petals and one of the women tried to squeeze past Mary to help Monica. As she reached for the fallen basket, she caught her shoe on the edge of Mary's veil, and the veil flew off Mary's head and landed on the floor like a delicate bird. Monica, determined to continue her walk down the aisle, stepped on the headpiece and crushed it. Mary and her father stopped. The overly helpful attendee had rushed back to her seat and Monica stood on the lace head garment. John watched as Mary's face broke into a beautifully compassionate smile. Mary picked up the veil and handed it to her father, handed the basket back to Monica, and returned to her father's side. The two continued their walk up the aisle to the music that never missed a note as if the whole thing had been just what they had practiced.

After the ceremony many people went to the reception at Mrs. Smith's for the cake-cutting ritual and other customary activities. As the reception was winding down, John found himself with Jake and Wayne McLaughlin. To John's amazement, McLaughlin spoke of new business problems that Nestlé was having.

"John, this is probably not the time to tell you this,

but I must. Our company is facing some difficulties that may affect the very existence of our plant. As you know, we have recently completed some cost cutting-measures with our recent upgrading and mechanization. It will be my sad duty to let some employees go next week. Because of the unanticipated lack of milk production, these cuts may keep our business going for the next few months. I'm not sure how much longer Nestlé can stay in operation. If we should be hit with any other unforeseen misfortunes then the Bandon plant will probably fold."

"I thought with the end of the league that business would really prosper," John said.

"So did everyone else, so for now we must hope that milk production keeps up with our demand," Wayne said.

After the reception, John and Mary were ushered out of the boarding house amid people showering them with rice and flowers. They were off to their honeymoon site at Port Orford in the Bennett's Chevrolet.

Blakely   The Heirloom

Chapter 29

"Why don't you go in to town and talk to Frank and River. I'll stay and work here. With your hat pulled down and that beard of yours, no one will recognize you," Matt said.

"I'd like to get our second installment of money myself. I'm tired of throwing yeast and refuse into the flume. I'll also be able to find out if our work has had any effect at Nestlé," Luther said.

Luther headed off down the hill to Bandon. His destination was the speakeasy in the Oriental building, and some fun in the rooms above. He entered the large empty dance hall through a small door. His footsteps echoed against the walls, and then he opened another door that led to the private bar. This room was dark and he could barely make out where the bar was located. As his eyes adjusted to the low light, Luther saw two groups of men seated at tables. Luther went directly to the bar, ordered whiskey, and then asked the bartender to direct him to Frank and River. The bartender pointed to a table in the corner with a dim light overhead where two men were sitting. Luther grabbed a chair and carried it over to the table.

The two men were small in stature and they wore cowboy hats. They had small shot glasses of whiskey in front of them. "Matt told me to look you guys up. He said you would have our second installment of money. We've been doing as you asked," Luther said.

River replied, "We don't have any money today." As soon as the words left his lips, Luther had the man by the collar and pulled him out of his seat holding him in the air. His cowboy hat dropped to the floor and his boots dangled two inches off the ground. River couldn't speak because of Luther's grasp. Frank yelled, "Hold on before you kill him. Let him down now!"

"I'll let him down when I get my money," Luther growled.

"We can explain if you will let us, now let him down!" Frank said.

Luther relaxed his grip and sat River back in his seat.

"Hold the noise down!" The bartender nodded to Luther. He was a big man, as large as Luther. "If I hear one more outburst like that I'll throw you out."

Regaining his composure and putting his hat back on, River gasped, "Before we can pay you we have to have some evidence that the condensary is affected. Our bosses won't pay us until they see some results."

Frank chimed in, "That's what we told Matt, we must see results."

Luther stared at Frank. "I'll let it go for now, but we've been doing the work, and we expect money the next time I come in. Tell your bosses that, for me, OK?

"Yes, yes, we'll tell them," Frank said. "We do have another way you can make some money. How is your brew supply?"

"We've got lots of the stuff, why?" Luther said.

"There's a whiskey runner due in port next week. They need merchandise. Would you sell to them?"

"What's in it for us?" Luther responded.

"Money," Frank said. "Lots of money."

"What about the authorities?" Luther said.

"Once we get the stuff on the ship, we're safe. The Coast Guard captain has already been bought."

"OK, then we will bring our whiskey to town when you tell us." Luther said. "Now, what about the women upstairs? How do I make arrangements?"

River said, "You're in free this time. Go on upstairs; I'll let the bartender know it's all right." River got up and went over to the bartender, pointing at Luther. The bartender nodded at Luther. Luther finished his drink and went upstairs.

Blakely

The Heirloom

Chapter 30

Earl and Mark stood on the bow of the ship looking out to the horizon. Waves were cresting in the choppy waters. Earl could feel the bounce of the ship as she thudded through them. Frank Helmuth came over to the men and shouted, "We're sailing south directly for Cape Horn. We should be reaching the equator soon."

A sailor walked toward the men, dragging a kicking and screaming young boy. "Look what I found hiding with our live animals. He was hiding behind two bales of hay." The lad looked up sheepishly at Frank.

"How long have you been hiding down there?" Frank asked.

The stowaway trembled, "Since we left New York, sir."

"What's your name lad, and how old are you?"

"I'm ten and my name is Joseph."

"Joseph, you have gotten yourself into a fine mess but I think we can work things out. This is what I want you to do. Earl here will take you to the sail maker. The sail maker will give you some clean clothes and show you how to take a bath. After that you will report to the cook. You will be working for him for the rest of the voyage. And Joseph, if you do not do as the cook instructs, then Cook will throw you overboard for the sharks' dinner. Do you understand, young man?"

"Yes sir, yes sir," said the frightened lad.

Earl took Joseph by the hand and deposited him with the sail maker, and then returned to the ship's rail to watch the sea. Albatrosses sat on the ocean for miles around creating a sea of white. As the ship sailed through the birds they would clumsily fly from the water, but once airborne they were the most graceful birds Earl had ever seen. He was astounded at their huge wing span and delighted in seeing them as they flew over and around the ship. Earl watched as flying fish popped out of the water, flew as if to take off and then dove back into the sea. The ship had had an unexpectedly easy voyage. The wind filled the sails and the barometer was holding steady.

Mark came over to Earl's side of the ship. "Have you heard of the Neptune Ceremony?" he asked.

"No," Earl responded.

"I've read that sailors who haven't crossed the equator are made to go through an initiation ceremony. We're nearing the equator, so be alert," Mark said.

The next day Earl was on deck and noticed that it seemed deserted. Where is everyone, he thought. Just then, a scarf was placed over his eyes and before he could grab his knife from his scabbard, his wrists were locked in handcuffs behind his back.

"What's going on here?" Earl said.

"We plan to make you a Shellback," a crewman said, reeking of rum. Earl was pushed across deck to another part of the ship and forced into a chair.

"Take these handcuffs off!" Earl thought he recognized Douglas Gilbertson's voice. "When I'm released I will put the lot of you in chains and keep you in the cargo area 'til you rot." On the other side he heard Joseph crying.

"Don't worry, Joseph," Earl whispered, "This is just a game, you won't be hurt."

Earl could see out from under his blindfold and saw two other crew members seated and blindfolded. Eric

Hansen stood before Doug with a crown on his head and a large staff in one hand. Next to him was Frank Helmuth in a woman's dress and a queen's tiara on his head. Behind those two were the rest of the crew, dressed in ridiculous costumes; some were naked. Most held pots and pans in their hands and there was a fiddle player and a man who was playing the harmonica.

On the king's command, music filled the air. The crew looked like a menagerie of musical figurines, all activated simultaneously by the wave of the king's hand. They banged out a loud repetitious noise that finally ended up with the fiddle playing a lively ditty. When the fiddler stopped, the king regained control.

"Stand up, Gilbertson," Hansen said. Earl could see Doug standing before the king, blindfolded and cuffed.

"How old are you?" Hansen asked.

Doug opened his mouth to answer, and one of the crew shoved a lathered shaving brush into his mouth. Doug spit soap. "That stuff is awful," Doug gargled.

"You didn't answer the question," King Neptune said. "Shave him!"

Doug was shoved back into his chair, and his head and chest were shaved clean while the improvised band clanged out their rendition of music. The music stopped and then Joseph was led before the King.

"What's the name of our ship?" The king said.

"I don't know," said the trembling lad.

"Shave him," said the king.

Next was Earl.

"What's the name of the woman you love?" the King said

"Mary," Earl replied.

"Shave him," the King said.

As the music played it was clear to Earl that no one could say the "correct" answer. After they had been shaved the crew yelled, "Throw the lot of them overboard."

"Remove their cuffs and prepare the plank," Hansen said.

All five landlubbers were lined up and Earl was first into the water. He was climbing back over the rail after his plunge into the water and saw Joseph waiting his turn on the plank. Hansen put his staff in front of Joseph and prevented him from stepping further out the plank. "Not this one," Hansen said, and the boy was spared the ordeal.

After the four initiates climbed back on board, they were warmed with rum and made to swear that they would perform the same ceremony on new sailors when passing the equator. Earl gave Joseph a sip of rum. The rest of the day was passed in more fun and frivolity.

Earl watched and smiled to himself; Captain Hansen was taking a real liking to Joseph. The captain showed Joseph the ship and Earl saw him explain to the youth how everything worked. Joseph beamed because of all the attention the captain was devoting to him. When Earl questioned Joseph later, he was astounded at how much he already had learned. "A fine young man, a good attitude," Captain Hansen told Earl.

After the Neptune Ceremony it was back to business. The crew resumed their daily shifts; the cook returned to the kitchen and the sail maker to his quarters. Earl overheard Hansen talking to Joseph, "It won't be long before our ship is at the tip of South America, where the Atlantic Ocean and the Pacific Ocean collide. These are the harshest sailing conditions in the world. When we reach the Cape, the courage and endurance of each man will be tested."

Chapter 31

When John and Mary returned from their honeymoon, they took up residency at Bennett's dairy farm. John would take the ferry to work each morning and Mary helped her parents with chores. John was the happiest he had ever been, but he saw tears in Mary's eyes sometimes and wondered.

Finally, one morning he asked, "Mary, why are you crying?"

"I'm just so worried about Earl, I haven't heard from him in months." Out of habit John felt for his watch. How would Mary act if Earl did return, he worried. Did she marry me because of the baby? Does she even love me?

And if worrying about Mary and his marriage wasn't enough to fill his mind, he had a letter from Robert Crowe. He read it at the breakfast table:

John,

It's recently come to my attention that the Nestlé plant in Bandon is experiencing some major problems. Your Supervisor is probably not aware of it yet, but we have received many cases of canned milk that have spoiled in the can. They were returned to the San Francisco plant a week ago. We have been trying to figure out which plant is responsible. We determined yesterday that the bad batch is from Bandon. Wayne McLaughlin will be informed about this problem very soon. As you know, I have recently married, and both my wife (a former Bandon native) and I long to return. I have put in for the Bandon Superintendent's job. I think Wayne will be leaving soon. I look forward to renewing friendships with you and Jake. Maybe we can do some fishing, or play some basketball. Maybe we can win a championship this time around.

Your pal,

Robert

"Robert is coming back to town," John said as he sipped his morning coffee.

"He's coming back here to live?" Mary asked.

"Yes," John said," and he's bringing his new bride. Some of our plant's canned milk spoiled in the can. He's hoping he can find the problem and fix it before the company has to close our plant. If anyone can bolster this sagging business, he can. And if he can't, then Robert, Jake, and I will be looking for new jobs."

Mary spoke, "The stern-wheeler is coming; you'd better hurry." John rushed out the door and down the gangway, jumping on the ferry as it slowly steamed past.

As soon as he got to the plant he was asked to come into Wayne McLaughlin's office. "The San Francisco office has notified me that a thousand cans of spoiled milk have been returned to them. The company traced the bad product to our plant. There is a chemist on his way to inspect our process and find out why our condensed sweetened milk is turning bad after it leaves our plant. In the meantime, we will stop our milk supply above Coquille. Nestlé wants us to stop production on sweetened condensed milk. We will produce only whole condensed milk for the time being."

"Do you have any idea what is making the milk go bad?" John asked.

"I simply cannot figure it out. I am hopeful that the

chemist from San Francisco will discover the problem. He's due here tomorrow. Nestlé's administrators also informed me that Robert Crowe will be replacing me as Plant Superintendent. I'm headed back to the corporate offices in San Francisco. Mr. Crowe will be here soon."

John tried to contain his happiness at being united with his old friend, Robert. He went back to work.

The very next day the chemist from San Francisco, Harold Carter, arrived, and worked with Bandon's chemist, Ray Wilkins. While at lunch in the cafeteria, John was joined by Ray and Harold.

John was munching his sandwich as the two tossed theories back and forth. "I think it's something in the water supply. Something is making the sweetened canned milk ferment in the can," Harold said.

"But what? Our water supply is good, has been all along," said Ray.

"Maybe it's blackberries falling in the reservoir?"

"There's a lot of berries up there, but it seems like it would have to be a lot of berries to cause this kind of trouble. Besides, the berries have been growing along side the reservoir as long as we've been canning milk. Maybe someone's dumping something in Ferry Creek."

"You mean, on purpose?" Ray asked.

"What with Prohibition, could it be some moonshiners throwing mash in the creek?" John asked. "I've heard a lot of stories about the 'shiners in the hills outside of town. There's usually someone doing business out back of the Oriental whenever there's a dance."

"Without a good water supply, John, the plant cannot produce wholesome canned milk." Harold said. "Good clear water is the most important ingredient to canned milk."

John finished his sandwich, wondering if Robert

knew what he was getting himself into coming back to Bandon.

Three weeks later, Robert called John and Jake into his office.

"Bad news, fellows. Since the chemists determined that Ferry Creek Reservoir water is polluted, I've been busy trying to find another water source. The local well drillers confirm that there is not enough underground water to supply what we need."

"What's going to happen," Jake asked?

"The plant will close down," Robert said.

John thought how incredible it was that this business, the largest condensary in the United States, could close. Nestlé had been a real economic treasure for Bandon. It had raised the spirits of the local inhabitants by employing more than 120 people, helping dairy farmers to prosper, all in the span of a few years. John thought Nestlé would last forever, and it was crashing down in front of his eyes. "What's going to happen to the building and machinery," John asked?

"The machinery will be moved to other Nestlé plants. The building will be sold. I doubt if any food company would buy it since there isn't a good water source. The building could lie empty for years," Robert said. "We will close next Friday," Robert said, regretfully.

"We all have families to support so we'd better start looking for other work. I've heard the Coast Guard is in need of recruits," Jake added.

"Go check it out," John said excitedly.

That evening at the Bennett farm, John told Mary and her parents what Jake had found out. "The Bandon Coast Guard Unit is hiring recruits, so we are planning to apply tomorrow," John said.

"I've heard how dangerous that work can be. I don't want you to work where your life will be threatened," Mary said.

"Business and work opportunities are getting worse each day," John said. "I really don't think we have much of a choice. Besides, the three of us are in excellent physical health and we will make it through the arduous physical training."

"I've heard it's long hours, and you will be away from your family for up to six days at a stretch," Mrs. Bennett ventured.

"There are disadvantages with any job," John said. "Besides, Jake says it's a great opportunity. We will be saving lives and ships. I'm really excited about being a recruit, and working with my two friends. We'll watch out for each other."

Later that night, as he imagined the interview the next morning, John realized Mary had not said another word about the Coast Guard job. He wanted her acceptance and now he wasn't so sure he had it.

The next day the three basketball stars signed up as recruits in the United States Coast Guard.

Chapter 32

As the huge windjammer sailed south, Earl's hopes of returning to Bandon grew dim. The stories from the experienced sailors became more vivid. Earl wondered why on earth these men were going back to this torture that shattered nerves and broke spirits of the bravest. It was during one of those fretful wonderings that Captain Gilbertson invited Earl to dine with him and Captain Hansen.

The two captains and Earl sat at the big table in the captain's cabin. "Where's dinner?" said the hungry Doug.

"It'll be along shortly," said Hansen.

At the knock on the cabin door, Doug yelled, "Enter lad, we are starving." Earl got up and opened the door and in walked Joseph with a large tray of food.

"Joseph," said Captain Hansen, "I want you to join us for supper this evening." Joseph could not do anything but accept a direct order and seated himself, not looking at anyone. Earl watched as the hungry Joseph slurped up his meal.

After the meal, Doug took the sextant up on deck to work out their course. Earl listened as Joseph and the old Captain talked. Captain Hanson told Joseph stories of the ships he had directed around the Horn in earlier days, large windjammers filled with grain. "I've never lost a sailor, although I've seen my share of shipwrecks off the Cape. I think it's careless captains, and careless owners, who lose men. It's the captain's job to maintain order and on long voyages he earns his money." Earl watched Joseph's eyes grow big as Hanson's story progressed. These evening chats became a regular activity, and Earl was glad he was included. He enjoyed the old captain's stories as much as Joseph did, and he saw Hanson's affection for the boy, a father for Joseph and a son for Hanson. Earl reasoned they adored each other.

One evening while Earl was on deck, Doug told Earl he was pleased with this exceptional crew. "A long voyage like this can bring out the worst, complaints and fights. Sailors complain about the food, the weather, the officers. They'll fight amongst themselves, too. This crew is different. They're working together."

"One thing I hear from the sailors is that the officers listen to the men," said Earl. "I think the crew feels important and they realize it takes all of us to run the *Padal*," Earl added. It was this optimistic attitude that prevailed as the barometer began to drop and the clouds darkened as the ship sailed towards the tip of South America.

The weather continued to worsen. White waves crested higher and higher; the ship made it to the top of one wave only to descend into the deep gray valley of another. Earl felt as though he was on a sled coming down a steep incline. His stomach filled with butterflies on each descent. Rain began to fall and the temperature dropped. Icy winds made the sailors' jobs all the more difficult. Earl edged his way toward the captains near the helm, pulling himself along the railing. He could see Hansen's white beard as it fluttered over his right shoulder. Earl arrived just in time to hear the bearded Hansen shout, "The best way to challenge the Cape is to continue south and wait for the east winds to drive us north westerly. There is a danger to this, and that is if we go too far south we will end up in the Antarctic where the air is freezing and the water littered with icebergs. This way, we'll catch the winds coming from the east and they will propel us westward around the cape and push us north into the Pacific Ocean."

As the evening closed in, one star could still be seen in the northern sky. Earl watched as Doug moved off with his sextant to determine their direction so he could keep the ship on course. The star quickly faded from view as the dark clouds obscured the heavens. "Furl the top sails on the foremast, mainmast, and mizzenmast!" Doug hollered to the first officers who relayed the orders promptly to the sailors on that shift. Waves crashed over the railings and covered the deck of the ship. "Stretch the life lines on the decks!" screamed the first officers.

The four men ate supper in the Captains' quarters as the ship bobbed up and down like a cork. Doug had invited Earl and Mark to join him and the old Captain. Little Joseph was helping Cook this evening.

"Thousands of men have lost their lives on this passage," the old sea captain said. "I've seen sailors fall into the sea from yardarms, washed overboard by powerful waves, and crushed by masts that snapped off in the tornado-like winds. Loose gear has maimed and killed, and I've heard about entire crews that froze to death. Hundred of ships have simply disappeared." Earl caught his goblet before it slid off the table as he listened intently to the old captain.

"Prepare for the worst, take every precaution known to man, watch every step you take, hang on for your very dear lives. You will learn to respect the sea, for we are fast approaching an area were the sea has no pity on you, where the sea is in cahoots with the devil, and wants to drag you down. You MUST fight back and not give in to its relentless attack. Nowhere in the rest of your lives will you face the trials you are about to face. If you should survive, you will forever look back on this experience as a turning point that allowed you to pass; you will become men, and you will know something that most other men will never know." As if in a trance the old captain ranted on. "You'll know the force of the sea: it will exasperate you, threaten you to the point that you will wonder what on earth you ever did to deserve such punishment, and you will beseech God to save you. But know this: your ship is a good ship, it will survive the thunderous waves, the icy weather, the punishing storms, and the ships good end will depend on the character of its captain and crew to get it 'round the Horn and heading north to North America. We have to take care of the crew and keep the lines of communication open in the weeks to come. With order preserved, with the picture of a goal in mind, we will all prevail." With that, the old man, showing strain and exhaustion, got up left the table and retired to his bunk.

The three remaining men sat in silence. Finally, Doug said, "I, for one, plan on making it back to Coos Bay. Lucy and I plan to wed when I return. No iceberg, no foul weather, no storm or ship's frailty will keep me from her arms!"

Earl said, "I'm looking forward to seeing Mary. I wish now that I'd never left Bandon. I wish with all my heart I had married her. We grew up together sharing childish hopes and fears. I adore her, yet I've disgraced her. I must get back to Bandon. So, this is my dream now. I do not plan on perishing at sea."

Mark said, "Mother was right: I should never have taken this voyage. The dangers seem so great I wonder if I can live through them."

As the men talked of how they all planned on sailing through the storms, each revealed his innermost character. Nowhere on earth did men get to know each other in greater depth than at sea, facing adversity of every kind, sealed off from land for months on end. In these moments of profound reflection each would try to explain the meaning of their very existence. They would probably never experience this type of introspection again.

After dinner, a fierce storm swept down on the good ship *Padal*. The icy wind grew in intensity and blew twenty-foot waves over the ship in a smothering blanket of churning water. The ship trembled from the force but recovered each time and rose to the top of yet another wave only to sink back in another chasm and be brutalized again. The sea tried a hundred chaotic maneuvers to dismantle the helpless ship. The crew cowered in their bunks and hidden spots, and thrilled to a life's intensity some had never experienced before. To Earl it seemed that this endless storm would never stop.

He got down on his knees and prayed, "Almighty God, please keep me alive! I must get back to Mary."

The next morning the storm was still pounding the ship, hurling wind, rain, and snow. Doug told Earl that he had decided to sail through the storm. He ordered the first officers to have the men unfurl the fore and mainmasts sails. Earl watched as Mark, along with two others, climbed the towering spar and stood on icy ropes, working on the foremast sail. Earl saw that parts of the sails were frozen, and other parts were swollen with water, making the sail heavy and hard to manipulate. Icy water trickled down Earl's neck, and he hoped Mark would be careful. On deck, men worked the winch which pulled at the sail trying to raise it into place. It was the sailor's job, high up on the mast, to work the gaskets and lines loose to enable the winch to raise the heavy upper topgallant sail. The towering masts tipped from side to side in the huge rolling waves as the men worked feverishly.

Mark was having trouble keeping his balance. He was practically on the end of the yardarm. Earl wanted to yell at Mark to come back down. The huge ship would first lean portside then quickly lean to the starboard, tilting the huge masts almost horizontal to the sea. Earl watched in horror as Mark's feet went out from under him and he fell to a seated position on the icy yardarm. While holding on to the yard he struggled to get his feet under him. His hand got caught under one of the metal gaskets as the icy wind blew down on the ship, forcing the sails to bulge out. The gasket came down hard against the metal yardarm. Half of Mark's hand was instantly chopped off. He lost his balance and tumbled through the air, into the sea.

"Man overboard, man overboard!" Earl screamed. Doug grabbed a buoy and tossed it into the sea where Mark had gone into the water. "Lower the dinghy!" Doug shouted. "Swing the ship around!" he ordered the helmsman. Earl jumped into the life boat and two more sailors quickly joined him as it was lowered into the sea. As soon as the boat landed, the men began to row to where Mark had fallen. Earl directed the crew through the huge waves.

As the tiny craft rode the crest of a wave the men scanned the sea for Mark. Finally, Earl spotted him clinging to a buoy. "There he is!" Earl pointed to the port side. The men rowed frantically to where Earl was pointing. The three men struggled to pull Mark into the boat. Earl noticed Mark's bleeding hand. Earl tore off a leg of his pants to use as a tourniquet and quickly tied it around Mark's upper arm. Mark was trembling and barely alive.

A stretcher was lowered on ropes from the big ship. Earl and the men placed Mark on it and pushed from below as it was raised to the deck. Doug ordered the men to carry Mark to the captain's cabin. Earl had climbed up the ship's side and ran into the cabin to find Mark laid out on the central table.

"Stand back!" said Captain Hansen. "I'll tend to this matter. Boil some water and get me the medic's kit," he ordered. Once the boiling water was brought to him, Hanson dipped the medic's saw into the water and proceeded to cut off the rest of Mark's mangled hand. Earl looked away as the hand dropped to the floor. Hansen stitched up the stump. When he was finished, Hanson told Earl and two other crewmen to carry Mark to his cot with an ample supply of rum and whiskey.

Earl shivered as he helped the men retie the life boat to the ship. His cousin had just lost his hand and had nearly died. What a foolish trip they were on. How could he have been so stupid to sign on to this voyage? His hands were numb with cold, his teeth ached, and his wrists and neck were chafed raw from the stiff rain gear. Earl pushed Mark and the present out of his mind with memories of Bandon and Mary... and her sweet smile.

Chapter 33
The United States Coast Guard

John and his two friends passed the required physical examination performed by Bandon's Doc Armstrong and signed on for a year's enlistment in the Coast Guard. With their initial prerequisites complete, they would begin working the next day. Jake never let his two pals forget about his father's experience and how much he had taught Jake, and John and Robert looked to him as the expert.

It was about three in the afternoon and all three couples were gathered at Mrs. Smith's boarding house to eat a mid-afternoon supper. Robert introduced his new wife Amanda to the group. Mrs. Smith had taken charge of providing the meal, and John was fairly certain she hadn't started drinking yet. Amid the aromas of fried chicken, pie and coffee, the friends began to discuss their immediate future.

"My father received only one medal for all his heroic acts, and he deserved more. After one rescue he was in the hospital for three months. My mother told me he almost died. Two of his buddies drowned attempting to rescue passengers from a steamer that was going down." John noticed that Mary and Julia had glanced at each other, and Amanda was fidgeting. John got Jake's attention with an elbow to his ribs and nodded in Mary's direction. Just then, Mary slammed her fork on her plate. "Why have you men signed up for such dangerous work? We will be constantly worried about you!" John took a sip of coffee and said, "This is just a temporary job for me, until I find something else."

Robert had just swallowed a mouthful of potatoes when he said, "I have been reading about the Guard and it's a lot safer now then it used to be. I've signed up for a new correspondence class that the Coast Guard has just created for enlisted men like us. And Mary, the Coast Guard has the League of Coast Guard Women. It's an organization of Guardsmen's wives and it's specifically designed to give the wives a voice in the lives of their husbands."

"I don't care about all these new programs; I care about John and his staying alive," Mary said.

Mrs. Smith brought in pie and freshly brewed coffee and served everyone. Robert said, "Believe me Mary, it's not nearly as dangerous as it used to be. They're trying to make the Guard more attractive to qualified recruits like us by establishing a retirement program and programs that will increase morale." There didn't seem to be any magic words for the women. John knew by Mary's continued silence she had not changed her mind. The women were worried about the safety of their men, and that was that.

The next day John, Robert and Jake reported to the crew quarters building located on Bay Street. They entered the building and found themselves in the middle of a room lined with bunks on each wall, a foot locker at the end of each bunk. A massive table was in the center of the room. There was a kitchen at one end of the room with stove, ice box and sink. They were part of a nine-man crew plus the Warrant Officer.

Warrant Officer Evans had them all stand at attention and questioned the newcomers. "John Dowd, I know that last name. Was your father a police officer in Portland?"

"Yes, sir." John felt proud for his father and fought a smile. He looked into Evans' reddening face. Evan's stocky frame became erect, and his blue eyes narrowed to slits.

"He arrested me two times for crimes I didn't commit." John was surprised that Evans had such a high-pitched voice. Evans hissed, "Beware, do your work correctly. Any mistake you make will be reason enough for me to give you a dishonorable discharge. Remember, I'm Captain here, you forget that and you'll be discharged. Do you hear me, Recruit Dowd?"

"Yes, sir!" John said.

John found out later that day that most of the crew hated Evans. More than one man told him that the Bandon station had a large turnover of recruits in the two years since Evans' arrival. "He's kept on because he knows how to handle the most difficult life threatening situations. He trained at the mouth of the Columbia, and the water up there is the most dangerous on the West Coast. The District Commanding Officer thinks there is no seaman in Oregon with Evans' experience. So we're stuck with him."

That evening John chatted with the tall wiry Tom Bigalow. Bigalow's bunk was next to John's. "I loathe him. I keep a log of every incident with Evans. Writing it all down is a lot safer for me than telling him off. I'd like to yell in his face, but I don't want to be kicked out of the Guard." Tom reached into his footlocker and took out a notebook. "Some nights I write until the lights are out. I long for the day that imbecile will be replaced by Frank Thomsen. Frank's the Petty Officer, and I believe that Thomsen knows how to handle the men, and the crew respects him. When Captain Evans is away the Petty Officer assumes command and I have seen Thomsen in action many times. He's a much better leader."

"What are you writing about now?"

Tom said, "Two weeks ago we lost one of our best recruits. I believe Evans orchestrated his death when he found out the man had some damaging information against him."

"What kind of information?" John asked.

"We never found out because he was killed before he could tell any one. It happened while we were performing surf boat exercises in rough surf. Evans had just yelled at the man in that high-pitched voice to grab an oar. That's when the recruit whispered to me, 'I could end his career with what I know.' I looked up and Ted Burns was looking right at us. I think he must have heard what the kid had said. Burns and Evans are friends, and I think he must have repeated what the recruit said. The next thing I knew, Evans ordered the recruit to take up a very dangerous position as we tried to take the boat through the surf. The boat overturned, we all went into the water, and when I came up I saw that the stern had come down on the recruit's head, and his head was crushed. The death is still under investigation but I think it will be reported as an 'unfortunate accident'."

John had trouble going to sleep after learning about this death. At least it was clear to him why the crew seemed so drained.

Less than a week later, the men heard that the investigation into the accident found Captain Evans innocent; the unfortunate incident was deemed an accident, just like Tom had predicted. John worried that the results of the investigation would hurt the crew, but the arrival of the three basketball stars was making a difference. The crew's attitude was getting better. And as the crew did better, John found himself the brunt of attacks and harangues by Captain Evans. He did his best to not let the man get to him. John figured that Evans resented his presence. It seemed to John that every question he had was an excuse for Evans to yell at him. But the more Evans yelled at him, the more determined John was. He would not leave the Guard. John understood why Tom wrote pages and pages in his log every night.

Rules and regulations applied to every aspect of the men's duties. John was impressed with Robert because of how he had immersed himself in his correspondence courses, so much so, that he was becoming an authority on rules and regulations of the Guard.

One of those many duties was keeping watch for ships in distress at sea. By day the men would take four-hour shifts in the building located on Coquille Point. At night they would walk the beaches with their kerosene lanterns. They looked for anything suspicious, including ships too near the coastline or floundering on the jetty. They listened for screams of help during foggy weather. The Bandon crew was called on for emergencies on the sea, river and even in the town of Bandon. One of the first emergencies the new recruits were called on was to save a burning house on the east side of Main Street.

"Fire! Fire! Off of Main Street, hurry! Bring whatever tools you have." A citizen had run to the guard station for help. He was trying to rouse as many people as possible to help fight the blaze. "If the fire isn't doused, it will burn down the whole town!" The sleeping crew jumped out of their bunks and dressed quickly.

John said, "I'll take the shovels, Jake get the buckets, Robert grab the hoses." Two more men gathered gear and the five men ran toward the blaze. By the time they arrived, the house was completely engulfed. Robert yelled, "We must protect the neighboring houses. We'll set up bucket lines from the neighbor's wells!"

At one side of the burning house, Jake threw the buckets of water on the neighboring house as fast as buckets were handed to him, and John took the house on the other side of the blaze. As neighbors arrived, Robert assigned other jobs. The fight went on for hours, and at dawn the men knew they had contained the fire to a single house. As the sun rose, women served breakfast and coffee to the exhausted firefighters and the family whose house was still smoldering. The Thursday Bandon *Western World* stated:

Towns People, Led by the Guard Save Town

If it hadn't been for the quick action of our local Coast Guard Station crew, we might not have a town today. They led the townspeople in an all-out assault against the fire that rampaged the Cummings' home, which was completely destroyed. Mr. and Mrs. Cummings and their daughter are now staying at the Wilfords. The fire was caused by a burning candle left un-snuffed.

The next day, Captain Evans made no mention about his crews' heroic nights' work but instead roused them from their short rest to begin practice with the Lyle gun, an apparatus designed to shoot a life-saving rope to stranded vessels at sea, and which allowed the ships' crew an exit by climbing into a breeches buoy and then, one at a time, to slide down the rope to a waiting Coast Guard ship. The practice session would take all day, and was such an important part of a rescue that it would be practiced again on Monday.

Captain Evans had sent one recruit ahead to make sure that the large simulated ship's mast was still standing in the sand. Then he led the remaining eight men to the shed that housed the Lyle gun and associated paraphernalia. "Jeremy, prop open the double doors so that we can get the cart out." John watched as Jeremy, the newest hire, fumbled with the latch on one of the doors. "Not that way, stupid, do I have to show you everything?" Evans pushed the recruit out of the way and propped the door open himself. "Now do you think you can remember that?"

"Remember, men, this all has to be done in the allotted time. We will practice this again and again until we get it done correctly. Men, take your stations!"

Two long poles extended from the cart. Robert, Tom and Frank got on one side and Jake plus two others on the other. "Pull!" yelled the captain, and the six men pulled the large cart out of the shed running off at a trot. Jeremy and John took up their positions at the rear to push.

"John, I don't know if I can take much more of this treatment from our captain," gasped Jeremy.

"He talks to all of us like that. Try not to take it personally, just keep doing the best you can." The cart was moving along at a nice clip when Jeremy slipped and fell.

"Get up and get moving!" shouted the bulky captain. Jeremy struggled to get up and finally caught up with the cart. He had just started pushing when he fell again. "You clumsy oaf," yelled the Captain.

"If you can't catch up and do your share, you will be dismissed." The irate Evans grabbed Jeremy by the back of the head and viciously pushed him forward.

Jeremy dropped to the ground again. John sprang in between the two and ended up face to face with the Captain. Robert and Jake stopped pulling on the cart and rushed to where the two stood. They grabbed John and pulled him to the side.

"You are dismissed!" Jeremy stood for a moment in shock and then Evans turned to John, who was held fast by his friends. "If you ever get in the way of my command again, I will dismiss you as well. Do you hear me, mate?" the Captain yelled.

Prodded by Robert and Jake, John answered, "Yes…Sir."

The guardsmen pulled and pushed the cart to its designated spot where they could see the mast. John unloaded the cannon from the cart, accompanied by the Captain bellowing orders. "Robert, you get the gun powder. Jake, you get the box with the rope. Tom, the block and hawsers, Frank, the breeches buoy." The crew assembled the Lyle gun to be shot. John put in the gunpowder, and Robert inserted a lead cylinder that was attached to the rope in the faking box.

"Faster, faster," hollered the Captain. "This is taking too long, come on mates, let's shoot the rope over the yardarm now."

Robert ignited the fuse. "Stand back!" Robert shouted, "Stand back, get out from behind the cannon." BANG! The cannon resounded and sprang backwards six or seven feet. The lead cylinder hurtled through space in a perfect arc over the yardarm. The crewman who had been sent ahead secured the rope to the mast. The breeches buoy was sent up the rope and the crewman climbed into the breech and was lowered to a safe spot on the sand near the cannon.

"Too long," said the Captain, looking at his watch. "We have to do it faster. Again, we'll do it until we get it right." By the end of the day, the men were exhausted and had failed to complete the drill in the time the Captain insisted upon. They returned to their quarters, and after their evening meal they all settled in, reading, playing cards, and quietly talking. John was doing his four-hour tour on the beach. Tom Bigalow wrote in his diary.

Tom's diary was getting a workout recording the happenings that occurred, because, except for Sunday, the recruits had to work every day. Mondays and Thursdays were spent with the Lyle gun; Tuesdays were spent training with the boats: the big oared surf boat, the motorized launch and simpler boats. Wednesdays were spent practicing signaling. They used large red and white flags to signal messages and the practice was called "Wig Wag." Plus, they practiced Morse code and proper radio procedures. On Fridays, Doc Armstrong taught first aid and life saving techniques. Saturdays were spent in cleaning the barracks and caring for the boats in the basement. Sunday was their day off.

John spent Sundays at the dairy with Mary, and he told her of the frustrations he was experiencing with the Captain. John had hoped to spend more time with Mary, but Captain Evans was forever finding some fault with his performance. "John, if you don't learn how to tie the knots, you'll have to spend Sundays learning them." Or, "Your footlocker is not clean enough." John spent too many Sundays at the station, and he didn't like it at all. Mary decided to write the district commanding officer and got signatures of support from Julia and Amanda.

On those Sundays when he was alone at the station, his mind worked overtime, worrying about Mary, the baby, and Earl's inevitable return. He would pull out his watch and gaze at it, flip up the cover and look at the inscription; he depended on this watch, it was his heritage, it was his comfort in time of trouble, it was his mother and father and the inscription never failed to inspire him. The touch calmed him. He was certain the watch would see him through the tough times.

Chapter 34
A Tragedy at Sea

Along with his aching wrists and neck, Earl's fingers felt frozen stiff. They were blue and numb yet he still needed to complete his chores. He knew every other sailor was suffering from the cold. Mark could no longer climb the shrouds, so Captain Gilbertson stationed him at the helm. For weeks Earl and the crew faced the icy winds, the snow and ice, turbulent seas, waves crashing over the rails, cold food, and sodden clothing.

Earl entered the crews' sleeping quarters. Men rolled out of their bunk to dress for duty and some, like Earl, were coming in for their cherished few hours of sleep. Some men staggered as the ship rose and fell. Mark was getting ready for duty at the helm, struggling to dress with one hand. Earl helped get Mark's pants fastened and then hung up his dripping oilskins and laid his undergarments at the tip of his bunk.

"I think the weather is clearing," Earl said.

One man showed his bloody fingers to Earl. The skin had cracked in the cold and wouldn't heal.

Earl put his arm around his taller cousin's shoulders. "Look, if you don't want to go out on this shift, I can handle it for you."

"You know that I've got to learn to cope with one hand, I'll be all right. I have cursed this ship, you, and the captain, and I have cursed myself for taking this trip but it really hasn't helped much. I'm sorry for being so mad but I think now I will be able to handle this." He held his wrist up and looked at where his hand had been. The skin was almost healed over the stump. "I have to get over my grief or I will perish out here," Mark said.

Earl marveled at his cousin's resilience. He thought, what would Mary think of me if I returned with only one hand? Mark was his inspiration because the man has shown such determination throughout the voyage, his accident, everything. The voyage is far from over, he thought, what else will happen to us?

While Earl slept and Mark assumed the helmsman's position, the weather calmed. Doug passed control of the ship to Captain Hansen. Ahead of them lay the most treacherous part of the journey.

They were sailing south when a sailor perched high up on the mast yelled, "Icebergs off the port side." Huge mammoth icebergs loomed off in the distance.

Captain Hansen ordered Mark to keep her to starboard. Slowly the ship assumed a westerly direction and the winds kicked up and pushed the ship west.

When Earl came up from his sleep he found Mark with a big smile on his face. "Earl, this is great fun, steering this ship through these icebergs." Earl's eyes almost popped looking up at the huge bergs. "Gently to starboard," the Captain said.

For a few days the ship sailed alongside the bergs and then sailed northwest, leaving the hulking masses to their own special solitude. Captain Hansen knew that soon the full force of the west winds would blow directly at them and that, in order to sail north, he would have to tack through them. Once the *Padal* was past these westerlies, the direction of the wind would be favorable and he could relinquish his command back to Doug. Until then, Captain Hansen worked around the clock directing the ship against the elements. On his shifts, Earl would see Doug at the old Captain's side. Weather conditions were getting worse; the barometer was dropping and the Captains and crew knew that they were in for a fierce battle.

After a rigorous day's work, the two men retired to the captain's quarters for their regular evening meal. They invited Earl to join them and as usual, Joseph brought in the meal and ate with them. The ship rolled and trembled from side to side as the four sailors ate their meal. The old captain wasn't as lively as usual. Earl saw that he was desperately tired from putting in so many hours without sleep. Earl was still eating when Hansen dozed off at the table, his head lying on his arms.

Quietly, little Joseph gathered the dishes and put them in his carrying container. He said goodbye and climbed the stairs that led out onto the deck. Earl lingered over the last of his coffee, knowing his shift was coming up. As he trudged up the stairs, he heard a shriek.

"Man overboard, man overboard!" Doug followed Earl up on deck. The wind was fierce and waves crashed over the bow. The *Padal* was little more than a stick on the sea. The first person he saw was Mark, lashed to the helm. Earl was caught full force by another big wave, and swept towards the aft of the ship. He smacked against the rail with his legs washed out beneath him and the upper part of his torso above the rail, like a limp rag folded over a clothesline, his breath knocked out of him. Doug edged his way over and then helped him walk to the helm. "It's Joseph, isn't it?" Doug asked.

"He lost his grip on the lifeline and a wave took

him over the side so fast I barely saw him," Mark said.

Earl was slowly regaining his breath; through his half-opened eyes he saw Captain Hansen come up on deck. Mark had already started the turn that would bring the *Padal* back around to where Joseph had gone in the water. Two dinghies were lowered into the swirling sea, and Captain Hansen commanded one of them. For two hours the men searched, but the lad could not be found. Finally in exhaustion and despair the men returned to the *Padal*.

Earl, waiting the long two hours for the search, stayed at the rail and thought about the foolish, senseless voyage. It had sounded so grand, and now it was a disaster. Why had he left Mary? He'd left her, his family, his home, and for what? A fool, he thought, I'm a fool. I was nearly washed overboard myself. But I wasn't, and there must be a reason I didn't die today.

Captain Hansen looked old and fatigued as he climbed over the rail and back on deck of the windjammer. "If I had not fallen asleep this would never have happened," Captain Hansen said to Earl. "In all my trips around the Horn, I have never lost a man. Now I have just lost the most precious man of all, a lad in the prime of his life." Earl saw the old man's spirit was crushed, all in one horrible fleeting moment.

A despondent captain directed Mark to bring the ship around, and tack to the northwest. "Doug, I want you to bring me the boy's clothes from the crew's quarters and one day's ration of food. Earl, prepare the crew for a burial at sea." In less than a quarter hour, the crew assembled on the deck. The *Padal* tossed and bobbed on the sea as Captain Hansen's voice rose above the howling wind and crashing waves.

"As you all know, Little Joseph was washed overboard today. His clothes and one day's ration of food are being dropped into the sea to help his soul confront eternity. Joseph came to us as a stowaway to escape the oppressive conditions he was living in at home. But he also came to us because he wanted to experience the excitement of being a sailor and he wanted to explore foreign lands. Although young and inexperienced, he leaves us today as a trusted comrade. He served us with honor, dignity and courage. You men are the heart and soul of this ship. Keep vigilant, work hard and be very careful. I love every man here and I loved this boy as my own flesh and blood." Tired and overcome with sadness at the loss of his dear Joseph, Captain Hansen turned to Doug in front of the crew. "Doug, I am passing control of the ship back into your hands. We have come through the roughest waters that Cape Horn has to offer. I know you are tired, but you are young and strong and will be able to carry on. The men respect you; do not let them down. As for me I am going to the Captain's quarters and get some much needed rest." With that said the Captain left and descended the stairs to his waiting cot.

As the sea continued its relentless assault on the *Padal*, the old captain slept. He dreamt of the great age of windjammers, of his crews, his cargos and the exciting times that he had been fortunate to live through. Then his dream became ugly and he found himself in a mighty battle of supremacy with the sea. As each wave crashed over him he was barely able to poke his head through the crushing surf to get his breath. Then the sea worked him loose from his foothold and ruthlessly thrust him against the sand with unrelenting force. He was like a piece of ship's wreckage being continually pummeled by huge waves and utterly helpless as he was dashed against the rocks. He fought back with every ounce of energy that he could muster.

As he slept his body writhed and jumped; arms and legs flailed about in a helpless effort to restrain the sea. The harder he fought, the more he thrashed about; then, in one last desperate effort to break free of the sea's mighty barrage he bounded off of the bed and landed on the floor with a thud. Gradually, Captain Hansen came to his senses. His body throbbed and ached with pain and guilt at the loss of Joseph. He grabbed a chair and steadied himself in the rolling room, and slowly stood up. He grabbed a pencil off the captain's desk, then sat down at the large table and wrote. When he was done, he put the letter on his bed and put on his rain gear.

Captain Hansen ascended the stairs to the dark deck. As he stepped on deck it was as if the whole world had suddenly come alive. The wind blasted about him, the ship's canvasses flapped about, waves crashed over the rails, and the noise was deafening. He could make out the crewmen at their duties. Hansen walked to the bow of the ship and climbed over the rail, lowering himself to a position just above the torrential sea. The water pushed at his frame but the captain held fast like lichen on a rock. It would not be the sea that decided Captain Hansen's fate that day; that decision was his alone. Then he sprang from his perch and plunged into the sea.

Captain Gilbertson was doing a flawless job directing the windjammer through the raging sea, yet Earl could see sadness in his eyes. Earl and the crew had been working long hard hours, and now they were effectively holding the ship to its course when the young captain spoke, "I want to check on the old captain, Earl. He's sleeping in my cabin. Would you join me, please?" Doug opened the cabin door and they slowly walked down the few steps to the wood floor. Earl looked around as they entered the room. There was an eerie silence; the chandelier swayed back and forth with the rhythm of the waves. The floor tilted one way and then the other. The captain's bed was empty. Earl saw the note and handed it to Doug. He read the note aloud.

Doug,

The loss of little Joseph is more than I can stand. I simply should not have allowed this to happen. I blame myself and cannot live with this tragedy on my conscience.

We have sailed through the roughest waters and I am certain you can carry on with valor from here back to your home town. Treat your men with respect and they will return the favor. Please do not be affected by what I am about to do. It is a coward's act but really I have lived a long and exciting life. I love the sea and I hate the sea. My aching and grieving mind has decided it is now time for me to leave this world.

Respectfully,

Captain Hansen

Both men sat down on the bed. "Captain, the death of Joseph was just too much for Hansen. It was evident in the burial ceremony he led. I could tell it in the way his voice quivered and I could see the despair in his eyes. That boy's death along with the captain's age tipped the scales in favor of suicide," Earl said.

"Two deaths on my ship. What do I tell the crew now?" Doug wondered aloud.

Earl sat for a moment then said, "Captain Hansen said that this crew was the best crew he had ever worked with. All of us had faith in his decisions and followed every order he ever gave. These orders are what led us around the Horn. Every man aboard this ship felt that this man was his father. I think you must take full command now; there is no one else. It will be a true test of your leadership abilities to replace this beloved man. You must tell the crew at once what happened, because keeping the men united in their efforts will sail this ship to Coos Bay."

"Earl, assemble the crew," Doug ordered.

Earl found Mark and told him what was going on and then the two of them passed the word that another burial ceremony was about to begin. Doug ordered Sam to bring Hansen's belongings on deck. The sea was a little calmer. Doug stood on the aft deck and below him was the crew. The ship swayed on the undulating water.

"Earl, throw Captain's Hansen's things into the sea." And then, as Hansen's clothes floated on the waves Doug spoke, "Men, it is with a great anguish that I gather you here today. A trusted advisor and friend has perished at sea. He decided to take his own life. We all know that he was despondent over the death of his friend Joseph, and this was the event that pushed our beloved captain to commit suicide. He wanted you all to know that he felt it wasn't this event wholly that caused him to end his life, but that he had lived a full exciting life and it was simply his time to go. Once he made his decision our beloved captain acted upon it. He loved every one of you, and I'm sure that every man here loved him. Captain Hansen was a great man and it was a privilege to have served under his command.

"Men, this is the last burial at sea that I will tolerate. I do not want to lose another man. You are a special crew. Captain Hansen realized this and spoke about it many times. I, too, have known that your cohesion is extraordinary. I have never seen such a healthy attitude among a crew in my lifetime. It is this remarkable attitude that will help us sail this ship in a way that Captain Hansen would have been proud. And now I make this promise to you: I will not sleep, I will not rest, and I will work ceaselessly, until this ship rides with proud bearing into my hometown port of Coos Bay. Men, it is up to us to sail this ship home."

Tears trickled down Earl's cheeks. He had loved the old captain, and he mourned his death. He had relied on Hansen's wisdom to get them around the Horn, and now he was gone. Earl watched Captain Gilbertson as he left his aft position, taking control of the ship.

"Unfurl the sails!" Doug yelled. "First Mates, get your men up those shrouds. We're going home."

The thought of getting home brought new hope to Earl. Bandon lay straight ahead. He looked northward at that horizon and thought, that's where the hope of my life dwells, if only I'm not too late. Favorable winds filled the sails with life, and the *Padal*, with its masts bending northward, sailed towards Coos Bay.

Blakely   The Heirloom

Chapter 35

John would do whatever it took to be a member of the Bandon Coast Guard crew, and he knew that he would have to take the browbeatings of Captain Evans. The Captain had singled John out from the rest of the crew from the first comment about John's father and he had never for a minute let up. Evans must have seen John as some kind of threat, and John doubted he could do anything that would change Evans' mind.

The surfboat and unsinkable launch were ready in the bay of Bandon. The Guard crew would tip the boats over and get them upright, over and over. Townspeople gathered on the docks to cheer the crew and share the contents of decorated picnic baskets.

The crew tipped the surfboat over first. The men crawled back into the righted surfboat. "Dowd! You forgot to get the oar! Go get it, stupid!" John glanced at Evans' reddened face and dove into the water to retrieve the oar. Evans reached over the side toward John, who grabbed at his outstretched hand. Just when John thought he could pull himself back into the boat, Evans let go John's hand and John tumbled back into the surf. John heard laughter once he got his head above water. "You fool," the stocky captain said, and louder, "Why did you let go? You can climb in by yourself." John got back into the boat and had not sat down when he heard Evans yell, "Tip the boat over, men!" The boat went over again, its side nearly connecting with John's head. Everyone climbed aboard again. "When the boat spills, you're supposed to spring out, Dowd." Evans glared at John and said, "Let's try it again." It hurt all the more for John because he really did know the correct procedures for righting the boats. Evans had used his harshest words on John, and John knew he must look like a fool to everyone. Evans pushed the crew: improve, improve, or you will pay! "Nice work, Burns! If the rest of you sorry excuses worked like Ted here, we wouldn't have any problems." By the end of the afternoon, John was exhausted and chilled. The drill ended at 4 p.m. The crew joined the townspeople on the dock and finished off the food and drank a lot of hot coffee. Evans had his audience; he entertained the townspeople with jokes and stories.

Evans didn't let up on John. On Sundays, he assigned John to practice flag signaling and ordered him to chop firewood for the enlisted men's quarters. He put John on graveyard sea watch for weeks. John knew that Evans wanted him out of the Guard and this made John even more determined than ever to take everything Evans could dish out.

A fierce storm wreaked its vengeance on Bandon in November. John was walking the beach with his kerosene lantern. Huge waves were crashing and visibility was poor. He was thinking of being with Mary on Sunday when he thought he heard faint cries for help. "Help! Help! Please help us!" The cries came from out on the water. John marked the spot on the shore and ran to the enlisted men's quarters for help. Petty Officer Thomsen organized the men for the rescue and sent one man to call the Captain. The men worked at a feverish pace getting the boat out of the storage shed, onto the cart, and to the spot John had marked on the beach. No one could hear any calls now and the surf was rougher than before. Evans caught up to the crew.

"Put the boat in here," Evans said.

"The survivor's boat would have drifted north in this wind. We need to put our boat in further up the beach," Thomsen said.

"Are you disobeying my order?" Evans said. He and Thomsen were face to face.

"We don't have time to argue, Captain. I'm not disobeying your order, but I know the currents and we must go further north if we have any chance of a rescue." Evans didn't say anything for several seconds, as if weighing what the rest of the crew might think, seeing the two of them in complete disagreement.

"Why don't you lead us to where you think we should put in. And if you are wrong, you will be severely reprimanded. Do I make myself clear?"

"Yes sir," responded Thompson as he turned to lead the crew up the beach. "Here, this is where we should put in."

Evans took the lead then, and yelled to the men, "Grab hold of the sides of our boat! On the count of three, we rush the waves and take this boat out on the sea. One, two, three!" The men rushed at the wall of water coming at them. The front of the boat went up as it was torn from their grip. The boat was thrown back with such force that it rolled over and over on the sand. "Again," the captain ordered. "One, two, three!" Again the boat was slammed back on the sand by the angry waves. Robert barely escaped being crushed. The Captain was about to give up and call the rescue attempt off when John and Robert stepped forward.

"Grab the side of the boat!" John yelled over the

crashing surf. "Three men to a side, get ready to shove this beast through those waves, now! Yeeeaaaah!" John and Robert rallied the crew as they ran again at the oncoming waves. This time the extra surge of energy overcame the pounding surf and the crew succeeded in getting the boat beyond the waves. Each man strained to get the oars in the water and take the boat toward the voices John had heard. Evans hollered through cupped hand, "Row on, row on, lads!" The men yelled too, hoping to raise a call from whoever it was in distress. Finally, "Over here, over here." The faint voice came out of the thick fog.

"This way!" The crew rowed in the direction Robert was pointing. The yells for help got louder and louder. The fog lifted slightly and the rescuers found an upturned boat tossing in the sea. Three men clung to the sides of the boat as waves crashed over them. One at a time the exhausted men were pulled into the surfboat. Their eyes were wide open in their fright, they were shivering and shaking from the cold. "How long?" one man asked of the rescued sailors. "Forever," came the answer through chattering teeth. "We were nearly done in. If you hadn't come when you did, we'd have never lasted." Another said, "There were two others and they floated off in that direction," and he pointed out to sea.

The captain directed the crew to row out a little further, but the sea was getting rougher and the fog had returned. Evans directed the men to row back to the beach. "Captain, I heard someone out there!" said John.

"Row to the beach," Evans commanded.

John shouted, "No, wait, I hear him!" John stood and dove into the water towards were he had heard the plea for help.

Robert shouted, "Follow John!" The crew bent

their backs at the oars in an effort to keep up with the swimming image before them.

Evans ordered, "Row to shore, row to shore!" The crew continued rowing after John. John spotted the man in the foaming sea and took control of the struggling man, towing him back to the boat. Once in the boat, the man collapsed. John treaded water listening for another cry, but, save for the sea, there was no other voice to hear. He swam back to the boat and let his crewmates drag him aboard.

Evans directed the full rescue boat towards the shore and a safe landing. Dawn faintly lit the eastern sky as all the men rested on the beach. The storm had blown itself out and left a light rain.

"We come from the steamer *Beagle*. We had passengers and crew of about thirty-seven. We were on a return trip from Portland to San Francisco. We lost our bearings and she struck a large rock. The boat just split in two and began to sink. The five of us were lucky to be near a lifeboat when we hit the rock. We no more got the lifeboat unlashed and a huge wave came down on the five of us and over we went. Somehow we managed to hold on, I'll never know how, but we did. As we all scrambled to get into the lifeboat we saw the steamer sink out of sight. We could hear the screams of people as they were sucked underwater and dashed against the rocks. We didn't have any oars, and then a wave upended our craft. We were lucky the boat didn't sink. We owe our lives to you fellows."

Captain Evans had Jake take the survivors to the Coast Guard station so they could warm up and rest. Evans directed John and Robert back to the beach to watch for bodies. Evans and the rest of the crew returned the surfboat to its shed. John learned later that the captain had ordered the motorized launch out to look for survivors. They found no one, just wreckage and debris. It looked as though the four men were the only survivors. Later that morning, John found seven bodies washed up on the sand.

The next day, Robert told John what he had heard about the *Beagle*. "The captain and mates had been drinking heavily. They were loud and rude to the rest of the crew and passengers singing, yelling, cursing, and even fighting. The sober crew broke up the fight, but no one was piloting the ship and it veered off course. We know what happened after that."

Bandon Coast Guard Saves Crew

Men from our Coast Guard unit braved the storm and surf and brought four sailors to safety. John Dowd's sharp ears picked up the sailors' cries as he walked the beach on patrol during the storm. He and Robert Crowe demonstrated courage and leadership as they put their rescue surfboat into the ocean, a feat they practiced just a few weeks ago as we all watched from the dock. It is possible that without these two men the surfboat may have not put out to sea at all, as the storm was the worst we've seen here in recent memory. Dowd dove into the water and personally saved the last man who was near death.

"This is our job," Captain Evans said to the assembled men at the next meeting. "No credits will be handed out here, no matter how brave we acted. We will not single out individuals in this unit."

Over the next weeks, John began to think that the higher-ups were not aware of the details of the rescue. Petty Officer Thomsen was replaced with Ted Burns. John overheard Evans telling one of his superiors that he'd removed Thomsen because Thomsen had put the surfboat in the water too far north and that was the reason the fifth man had been lost. "Had Thomsen put in where I ordered him, that last man would be here today." When John heard this obvious lie, he finally believed that Evans would say anything to make himself look good. The crew knew that John and Robert had been instrumental in making the rescue a success. They agreed that Ted Burns was not the man they wanted in charge either; Burns was useless in an emergency. The wives of the crew, all members of the newly-formed League of Coast Guard Women, decided to take action and wrote to the Superintendent of the Coast Guard with a list of complaints about how their local unit was being run.

Chapter 36

Luther normally didn't like anybody, but he did like Matt: Matt made him laugh. Also, he had nursed him back to health, and Luther would never forget that. It seemed as though the only times Luther ever laughed it would be at something Matt did or said. Matt was his personal jester. Like the time Luther finally told Matt that he had slit Ben's throat, Matt had shrugged his shoulders and said, "Guess it was his time to die." Luther laughed so hard his guts ached. Or the time he said, "The only thing I would like more then killing John Dowd would be to rape Mary." Matt had replied, "Me first, boss." Again, Luther roared with laughter.

In camp one evening, while sipping from kegs of their latest batch of brew, Luther said, "One day we'll kill John and Mary, and when that day comes, it will be on our terms. They will beg and plead for their lives," Luther said as he tried to envision the scene.

"Yes, yes," Matt purred. "What then, boss?"

"We'll slit their throats and leave their naked bodies for the vultures," he said as he spit a big wad of whiskey into the air.

"Then what?" Matt cooed.

"With the money we've made from Frank and River, and the money from the whiskey sales, we'll buy the whorehouse and bar. We'll be able to move out of this filthy forest and into town. From then on, we'll be on easy street," Luther said.

Matt's head bobbed up and down, "I can hardly wait."

"We need to get a big shipment ready. I heard talk in town that there's a whiskey runner who's been steaming up and down the coast selling brew, and their supply is getting low. River told me to be ready by Monday night. They want to buy all we have."

"That only gives us a few days, boss," Matt said.

"Tomorrow I want you to go into town to see if you can buy back some brew from our dealers," Luther said. "If you can, we'll sell that along with what we have here to the boat captain," he added.

"First thing in the morning, boss," Matt said.

About noon the next day, Matt said goodbye to Luther and headed into town to buy up all the surplus whiskey he could find. He'd agreed with Luther that he would stash whatever he bought in their secret cache. Matt was supposed to return before dark. When he hadn't returned at sunset Luther became alarmed and whispered, "If he's not back by morning, I will go into town and find him."

Chapter 37

On a Sunday morning John and Mary talked at the kitchen table. "I have written," she said, "about Captain Evans' actions, especially related to keeping you at work for longer hours then the rest of the crew. I also mentioned how poor the morale is at the station."

"At the inquest concerning the sinking of the *Beagle*, the Coast Guard was praised. No one testified to the captain's poor decision, or of my rescue of the sailor," John reminded her.

"I'll write again, and my next letter will tell of these circumstances, too," Mary vowed.

"I read in a statement from the superintendent that the success of the latest incident confirmed his opinion that the men were obviously well-trained. And the credit went to Captain Evans, too. Unfortunately," John said, "there just isn't enough reliable evidence against Evans to get him removed, at least not for the present."

That evening, John got off the steamer and walked downtown, headed for the crewmens' quarters. On Main Street he saw someone he thought he knew, "That's Matt, no one else walks like that, and he's still wanted by the sheriff." John was startled to hear his own voice. Matt had walked into the grocery. John waited near the entrance and watched the small man through the dingy window. Matt came out, carrying a rather large sack with his good arm. John stepped in front of him.

"Well, if it isn't my old friend Matt," John said.

Matt dropped the whiskey and started running. John caught him and dragged him back to the grocery store. Matt pulled a knife as John was inspecting broken glass and the ruined whiskey. John looked up just as Matt sliced the air with his knife and connected with John's bicep. The knife felt like fire in his arm, and John had to let go of Matt. Matt took off, and John gave chase once more, tackling Matt right in the center of town. A group of people crowded around them. Again, Matt swung the knife at John, but he didn't connect. Both men were face to face, and just as Matt took another swing at John, someone off to John's left drew his gun and shot Matt. He crumpled in a heap and lay on the ground like a guinea sack of feed.

The blast rang in John's ears. The next thing he knew, the sheriff was standing next to him. "What happened here, John?" The sheriff asked.

"Matt might have killed me had it not been for Jesse here. Jesse shot him. Matt wasn't going to quit with that knife of his."

John continued to stand and look at the body in the street. The sheriff asked Jesse to give his side of the story and determined that John and Jesse were telling the truth. Matt was wanted, and he had been in possession of moonshine. The sheriff arranged for Matt's body to be taken to the morgue. Then he took John to Doc Armstrong's office where the arm was stitched and bandaged.

When he arrived at work he told Jake and Robert what had happened. Jake said, "You don't suppose Luther's still alive, too." Just then the radio crackled with an SOS call. Thomsen, who was now dispatching, announced to the crew: "A steamer is stuck on the sand north of town. Its lifeboats have been torn off.

The waves are too high to attempt swimming to shore. The skipper thought that high tide would wash them back out to sea, but they're stuck fast and the waves are getting larger, he says. He's asking for help."

"Assemble the crew at the boat house," Evans ordered Burns. Once assembled, Evans instructed John and Robert and two others to bring the breeches buoy equipment to the launch. The rest of you come with me. We'll get the launch ready." Once the launch was loaded it set out for the rescue. A tug close to the stranded ship was radioed to hold its position. As soon as the crew arrived on the scene, the breeches buoy equipment was unloaded and put on the tug. The men prepared the gun to shoot a line over the steamer's central mast.

"Stand back," shouted Robert, as he prepared to ignite the small cannon's fuse. The blast shot the lead cylinder high in the air but missed its target. The rope was recoiled and the cylinder placed back in the cannon. "Stand back," Robert repeated. This time it was a perfect shot with the rope falling over the mast. One at a time, the crew was removed from the stranded vessel, until only the captain remained. Reluctantly, he climbed into the breeches buoy and was brought from the ship to the tug.

John asked Evans, "What about the ship's cargo?"

"That's not our worry, just keep quiet about the cargo!" Evans said. "That's the ship owner's responsibility."

"When do we start the salvage operation?" Frank asked the captain.

Evans' face looked perplexed and John immediately grew suspicious because the Coast Guard always helped in salvage operations. At last, Evans said, "Tomorrow."

Weather conditions improved the next day, and the Coast Guard crew was ordered to bring all available oared boats to the beach nearest the stranded ship. The steamer's crew had already brought the cargo on deck and prepared to move it ashore. John and Robert rowed to the steamer. Boxes were lowered into their boat. Robert looked in one of the boxes and saw bottles of whiskey. He raised his eyebrows at John and said, "This cargo is illegal contraband. This ship is a whiskey runner and operating illegally in these waters. John, we have to do something, even if it means arresting these people. It is the Coast Guard's responsibility to enforce the Volstead Act. Prohibition is the law."

Back on shore, John and Robert reported the smuggled whiskey to Captain Evans, who seemed to downplay the whole episode. "Don't worry about it. We can get the whiskey dealers later. For now, let's get the stuff unloaded." Evans lowered his voice and said, "John, Robert, it will be worth it to the both of you if you will forget what you saw today. If you will forget it then there will be a large sum of money for you at my place this evening. Think it over; I'll be right back." He walked over to talk with the ship's captain.

John and Robert could not bring themselves to engage in illegal activity. They assembled the crew and told them what had happened, and what Evans had offered. "I think we should confiscate the whiskey, right now. The crew of the stranded ship should be arrested, every last one of them. Tom, go to town and get the sheriff. And the revenue agent!" Robert said.

Burns couldn't believe his ears. He ran off and told Captain Evans what was happening. Evans raced back to the group. "This is insubordination! I will not tolerate John and Robert's behavior of not obeying my orders. Both of you are officially dismissed from service in the Coast Guard."

John said, his voice strong and controlled, "Captain, arrest the whiskey dealers." Evans took a swing at John, hitting him in the side of the head. John fell to the ground and Evans jumped on him, flailing his fists towards John's face. John deflected most of the blows, and finally pushed the heavy man off him. He scrambled onto Evans' prone body and locked the captain's hands behind his back.

"Get off me now! You, get this recruit off me!" No matter who Evans ordered, not one man stepped forward to interfere with John. "You are dismissed, you're all dismissed!" Evans' voice was hoarse. No one moved to help him, and John saw a few smiles. Even the recently promoted Petty Officer Ted Burns did not offer a hand in support of his benefactor. Burns apparently had sized up the situation quickly; the odds were stacked against him. John was handed some handcuffs and he snapped them into place on Evans' wrists. Robert stepped up to take command, and not just of this particular situation. He ordered the whiskey confiscated and three of the ringleaders cuffed.

By the time Tom arrived with the sheriff, Robert had everything well in hand. John had arranged for the whiskey to be delivered to the Coast Guard station.

"I guess those correspondence courses have really given you a command of the current laws. I'm proud to work under your leadership," said John.

"We have done the right thing here, plus it looks like our noble captain was taking bribes. Whiskey runners will no longer be welcome in our waters," Robert said. The handcuffed men were led off to jail by the sheriff and the revenue agent.

John, Robert and Jake were not too popular with

the moonshine producers and distributors. However, the townspeople grew to respect the quick decisions made by the three basketball stars.

Once the Coast Guard Superintendent reviewed the incident, he determined that Captain Evans had accepted bribes from the whiskey runners. Evans was court marshaled. Robert was appointed Captain by the superintendent, and Robert immediately appointed John, Jake and Fred Thomsen as Petty Officers. Ted Burns found himself demoted back to the enlisted ranks. Once Evans was gone, the morale at the Bandon Coast Guard station improved enormously. Robert restored order, respect, and set about making the station a place were the enlisted men could be proud they were serving.

John was a lot happier, too. No more spending so much time on the graveyard shift, and more time to spend with his beloved wife Mary. The Women's league sponsored several social gatherings for the men every month. The three friends and their wives were especially happy. Everything was working out, finally.

Chapter 38

A Sailing Feat

An uneasy pleasantness struck Earl as their windjammer reached the Oregon coast. They had sailed north from South America to the North American continent. The winds had been extremely favorable for most of the trip. Tacking through some fierce headwinds reminded Earl that the weather could change seemingly on a whim. Earl came to believe the voyage was chaperoned by two angels who cleared the way through the clouds and fog, angels who calmed the sea for the *Padal*. Earl gazed at the Oregon coastline, and spotted familiar landmarks on the way north, the Rogue River jetties, Humbug Mountain, Cape Blanco, and then Coquille Point. As they glided past Cape Arago, the lighthouse came into view. Earl knew now that they were truly home, for not far off lay the jetties of Coos Bay harbor.

"I have an urge to sail this ship over the bar, into the harbor and right up to the docks. I know our crew can handle it, and the winds are favorable."

"Doug, I'm with you. Let's make an impressive entrance! Coos Bay here we come!" Earl said. Doug radioed ahead to let the Harbormaster know they were coming in, knowing the whole town would show up just to watch the fully-rigged windjammer cross the bar. Doug ordered all the sails unfurled, knowing that catching the wind would take the *Padal* over the bar and into the harbor. If the wind died down, the Padal would be helpless against the strong sea currents.

Earl and his crewmates raced up the foremast, others scampered up the rear masts. Mark stayed at the helm position, taking orders from Doug. The strong wind tore at Earl's hair and clothes. He looked with trepidation at the fast-approaching bar and envisioned Mary, a ghost-like image, shimmering in the harbor. The great ship sailed directly at the turbulent bar, exploding over it and through the churning water. Miraculously, she found her way between the jetties that protected the harbor. Over the roar of the sea, the *Padal's* crew could hear cheers from the townspeople who were lining the harbor to witness the arrival of the magnificent windjammer, a sight that was becoming history too quickly. The crew furled the sails as the ship slowly came to rest near the docks.

"Doug, they'll talk about this for the rest of their lives!" Earl watched in amazement. He didn't know there were so many people living in Coos Bay.

The captain of a tugboat proudly steamed over to meet the *Padal*, caught hold of the ship and pulled it to a berth. With the great ship docked, the residents crowded around the pier and cheered the daring sailors.

Doug positioned himself on the aft deck. He asked Earl to call the men because he had something to say. Earl saluted and called the crew. "Before I allow you to debark I have a few words." Earl saw the tears swelling up in the Captain's eyes. Doug could barely speak.

"I am so proud of every one of you. I've never seen a crew work together like you did. We took on a dangerous voyage, and just when I feared we would fail because I lacked the experience of the old captain, you pulled together and brought us from New York,

around the tip of South America, and home to Coos
Bay. We faced adversity of every kind yet we prevailed
and pulled off an ambitious undertaking. It has been
a grand journey. My only regret is the loss of our two
comrades." To a man, the crew interrupted Doug's
speech with applause. "I gratefully thank every last
one of you for the fine work you have done. For
those of you who wish to stay in this area, there are
jobs for you at my father's lumber mill. For those of
you who want to sail on, you will receive my highest
recommendations. And don't plan anything for
tomorrow night. You are all invited to a big celebration
at my father's home! One last thing, two weeks' pay
and two weeks lodging in Coos Bay's finest hotel.
Thanks, one and all." The entire crew let out a loud
cheer. Doug stepped down from his perch and sought
out Earl and Mark.

"Come and stay with my family for as long as you
want," Doug said.

"I must get to Bandon. I can't wait any longer; I
have to see Mary," Earl said.

"What's two days when we have been gone for
so long? Come and stay through the big feast we are
having tomorrow night," Doug said.

"I must get to Bandon," Earl replied.

All three walked down the plank to the docks.
Doug's fiancée, Lucy, waved and let Doug enfold her
in his arms. Earl watched the long kiss. "Ah, fellows,
this is Lucy. I guess you figured that out already." Doug
introduced his family to Earl and Mark. Earl shook
hands with Doug's father, grandfather, embraced his
mother, and met Doug's sister Belinda, a stunning
blonde with bright sparkling big round blue eyes. She
looked all of twenty. Earl noticed Mark and Belinda
eyeing each another. Doug's parents insisted that his

two friends come to their home, and the men gathered up what they would need for the stay and headed toward the waiting cars. Doug's father spoke to Doug and Earl, away from the crowd. "It's fortunate you arrived today for tomorrow the barometer is indicating a huge storm."

"In that case, Earl, you're going to have to stay until the storm passes," Doug said.

"All right, I'll stay through the feast, but come the next day I'll be leaving early for Bandon, storm or not," Earl said.

Doug's grandfather asked about his old friend Captain Hansen. Earl saw the strain in Doug's demeanor and heard the tremor in his voice as Doug recounted the unfortunate circumstances surrounding the Captain's death. Earl watched as Doug regained his composure, then he abruptly returned to the *Padal* and gave orders for its care, shook hands with the crew that would stay aboard, and reminded them of the party.

Doug Gilbertson's folks were the descendents of one of the largest boat builders in the area, and Doug's father, Dwight, had carried on the boat building business for a while, then sold it in order to start a lumber mill that he was more interested in. The mill had been a great success, and was the largest one in Coos County.

After living in the tight crew quarters of the *Padal* for the last several months, Earl was amazed at the luxurious timber baron's house. It was three-stories tall, and perched on a cliff that overlooked the ocean. Earl and Mark were taken through the house and led upstairs to their bedrooms. Each bedroom had its own bath, fireplace and view of the ocean. The sea-weary Earl threw back the covers of the inviting bed, curled up and sank into a deep sleep, and dreamed of conquering, once again, the rough seas of Cape Horn.

During the night Earl awoke to raindrops hitting the window panes so hard he thought the glass would shatter. Not wanting to be disturbed, he pulled the comforter over his head and slept again. It was midday when he finally descended the stairs. He found the preparations well underway for the evening's crowd, the dining room table already set. The crew trickled in and by six o'clock the house was filled with family and friends. As the celebrants were seated for dinner, the wind gusted against the house and reminded everyone the storm was not yet over.

About halfway through the meal, conversation stopped suddenly. The diners watched through the window that faced the sea as a Douglas fir blew over in the violent wind. The ancient tree fell away from the house, flattening everything in its path, leaving its giant root ball exposed. Earl thought about how quickly the giant tree had tumbled. Was it a bad omen? Maybe he should just move up to Portland and find a job. Why did he have to see Mary again? He couldn't shake the feeling that his love for Mary was rooted far deeper than any tree, and that nothing could take that love away. If nothing else, he must seek Mary's forgiveness. The turbulence outside brought Earl back to the dinner table.

Spread out on the huge table was a bountiful supply of freshly prepared foods: platters of venison, beef, duck and salmon. Earl could almost taste the food as he smelled the wonderful aromas. There were large bowls of steaming vegetables, a variety of green salads and mashed potatoes. Each setting contained more forks than Earl had ever seen, and each place was adorned with a crystal wine glass. Light from the candelabras danced on the china, silver, and crystal. Outside the storm raged.

Earl and Mark were seated next to each other. Mark spooned up a variety of foods on his plate. Earl shoved a fork full of roasted duck into his mouth and washed it down with a half glass of wine. Earl dreamed he was with his beautiful Mary on their cliff hideaway as he filled his plate. He would see her soon, he vowed, he would be patient.

"Did you ever dream we would be eating this lavishly?" Mark asked.

Earl poured another glass of wine and said, "I wish tonight was over."

Earl watched Mark wink at Belinda across the table from him. Belinda smiled back. Earl smacked Mark in the arm with his elbow and said, "Tomorrow the first thing I'll do while in Bandon is to telegraph your parents about our safe arrival. Are you going to be traveling home soon?"

"I think I will stick around here for awhile. I think I'd like to get to know Belinda better, and I like the idea of work at Gilbertson's saw mill. Just tell them for me that it will be quite some time before I return home. Tell them I will write." Earl gnawed at a duck wing.

Peering between the candles Earl could see Doug and Lucy. They were really enjoying themselves and making up for the lost time they had been apart. He watched as they kissed each other's cheeks, smiled a lot and whispered in the other's ear. When he bent down to retrieve his dropped napkin, he noticed their tightly held hands under the table. Earl had never seen Doug so happy, and he felt empty, and maybe a little jealous. It seemed that all around him people were happy, and he wanted to be happy, too.

The sailors began telling stories about their exploits while sailing around the Horn. They talked of the Neptune ceremony and rough seas and the bitter cold. Officer Knudsen retold the story of how Captain Hansen took control of the great sailing ship and beat the steamer in a race. The men spoke fondly of Joseph, of their respect for Captain Hansen, how the two had become such good friends, and their tragic loss at sea.

Doug's grandfather stood at his place at the foot of the table and raised his goblet, "I propose a toast in honor of our good friends, Captain Hansen and little Joseph." Everyone at the table rose in quiet solemnity. "They were sailors of the highest rank, filled with boldness and courage. May God have mercy on them." The wind raged against the window. Earl felt his own tears fill his eyes and saw wet cheeks on the sailors around the table. Everyone took a drink of wine. The old man refilled his glass and raised it again. "My next toast is to you men who successfully sailed around the Horn and brought my grandson safely back to Coos Bay." He cleared his throat and spoke again. "My grandson tells me this is the greatest crew sailing any ship. I salute you for a job well done." The rest of the evening passed, filled with wine, stories, and toasts. The storm outside increased in its ferocity, reaching gale force. Rain pounded the house.

Grandfather Gilbertson decided that the crew would have to spend the night at the mansion rather then risk traveling back to Coos Bay. Makeshift beds were arranged, and as the crew and family made their way to bed, the wind broke trees and made the house shudder.

Blakely   The Heirloom

Chapter 39

The Storm

The fierce storm thundered against Oregon's southern coast. Tom Bigalow was acting dispatcher at the Coast Guard Station in Bandon. He'd already received a distress call from a boat caught on the rocks on the north jetty. He was planning a rescue with Robert and the rest of the men. Just then, a man ran into Tom's office. "There's a ship in trouble on the jetty, the waves are crashing over it. It's a schooner loaded with logs. The crew is trying to get off the boat. I saw one man slammed against the rocks as he tried to jump from the boat to the jetty."

"John, Jake, plus you three, come with me to the launch. We'll see if we can help that ship," Robert said.

"I've lost contact with the ship," Tom said before the rescue crew left.

The launch was readied and the three basketball stars plus three guard members pushed the boat down the rails, jumping in at the last minute. Waves slammed into the launch, making it difficult to maneuver. They managed to take the launch toward the stranded ship. John could see the ship's lifeboat tossing around in the water close to the doomed schooner. It looked to John like there were at least seven crewmen in the boat already, and they were begging the last man on the ship to jump. The sailor kept falling, losing his balance on the tossing ship. When he finally jumped toward the lifeboat, the impact of his landing threw the lifeboat over and the oncoming wave slammed them all against the rock jetty. John looked away, knowing that there was nothing to do now that would save the men. Robert ordered the launch back to the station. They would fish the bodies out when the storm had passed.

When the men returned to the station, they heard Tom yell, "I'm getting a call from the Coos Bay Coast Guard station. They've got several ships on their jetties. They want us to help with a ship that has crashed on Simpson's Reef. It's a big steamer that lost rudder control and it's on the rocks. If they don't get help soon the ship will sink," Tom said.

"Tom, try to contact ships near Simpson's Reef; I want them to stand by should we need their help. John, you and three men come with me," Robert said.

The crew launched again and made it through the highest waves on the bar. Out at sea, rain pounded down on them and huge waves crashed over the bow. It seemed an eternity before John was able to yell out, "There she is, to our starboard side!" The launch edged its way toward the stranded vessel. The captain of the stranded steamer had already responded to the order to let loose its reserve of oil, hoping to calm the surrounding water. Robert said, "John, all we know about the stranded ship is that there are thirty-seven people aboard and their life boats have all been washed loose." As the launch edged closer to the ship John could see panic gripping the boat's survivors.

"Look," John said. He pointed at the ship's mast. Several crewmen had climbed the mast and were hanging onto the yardarm as the sea crashed over the deck below. John didn't know how long they'd been holding on, but he imagined it had been a long time.

John watched helplessly as one man lost his grip and fell into the sea, disappearing. More crewmen jumped into the water, anticipating the imminent breaking up or sinking of their ship. The launch drew closer and John spotted a man struggling in the sea. John stood and handed his precious watch to Ted Burns who was sitting next to him. He dove into the churning sea and swam toward the drowning man. He reached the man and pulled him back to the launch. He brought two more sailors to the safety of the launch the same way.

Robert instructed the helmsman to get as near as possible to the wreck so that they could get some of the survivors aboard the launch. In spite of the churning sea and the reef, the launch got close enough that four more people were able to climb aboard. Robert saw a steamer waiting off the reef. He knew this was Tom's doing. The launch headed toward the waiting ship and transferred the rescued seamen.

Robert returned again and again to the wreck, until he was certain there was no one left to rescue. John dove in to frigid waters and saved another three men. All told, the Coast Guard crew saved twenty-two sailors. John saved six on his own. He rested against the side of the launch, drained of energy from his life-saving exertions. Robert, his eyebrows arched, looked at his friend in great admiration, as did the rest of the crew. "John, you will receive the highest Honor the Coast Guard can bestow. I will see to it," said Robert.

After the last survivor had been placed on the steamer in safety, Robert directed his men to take the launch home to Bandon. The waters were still treacherous and the launch rose and fell with each wave on its way back home. John could see the shoreline to the port side; he was tired and weary. He remembered his watch, given to Ted Burns for safekeeping, and asked for it back. Ted stood, watch in hand and leaned toward John. Just then a wave knocked into the launch and Ted lost his balance. He grabbed for the rail and dropped the watch. At the moment the watch hit the water, a ray of sunshine broke through the clouds and touched the gold, so brightly that John had to turn his eyes away from the glare. Exhausted, he still plunged into the rolling sea after his cherished heirloom and saw it become a silvery shadow, always just a few inches from his grasping hands. Deeper and deeper they spiraled down.

He remembered showing it to Mary on the stern-wheeler, and showing it to Jake and Julia at the boarding house, and how impressed they had been. He remembered the day the watch was given to him. He remembered the inscription inside of the lid, "In the confusion of life persevere." He had persevered and won Mary. He had looked forward to the time when he would give the watch to his son. Deeper and deeper they went. The watch was John's prized possession, it was a part of him, and he couldn't bear to lose it. Yet maybe, as Mary had said, he relied on the watch too much. He was so proud of this watch. What would comfort him in times of stress now? Deeper and deeper he swam until his energy was exhausted and he could go no farther. He watched helplessly as the heirloom spun away and out of sight in the murky water. From now on he would have to rely on himself; the only vestige of the heirloom that would remain was the inscription that was etched on John's brain.

Chapter 40

Earl Returns Home

Between the storm blasting away all night and his own excitement over his return to his hometown, Earl found sleep had been impossible. As morning arrived, Earl got up, dressed and went downstairs. When he entered the kitchen he found Doug already dressed and eating some toast. "Earl," Doug said, "would you like a ride into Bandon?"

"Yes, yes!" Earl blurted.

The two finished their coffee and then put on their rain gear. The wind was still blowing about forty miles per hour, driving the rain relentlessly. The two drove off in Doug's Model T Ford. Doug drove with caution, but all of the roads were mostly clear. To Earl it seemed like hours until they arrived on the outskirts of Bandon. The two friends shook hands as Earl got out of the car, closed the door and headed off to the center of town. Looking back he saw Doug's car fade from view in the heavy downpour.

Despite the storm, Earl felt good and was excited about returning to his hometown. The storm was a part of Bandon, too. He had loved this place as a child and he loved Mary. Earl found the telegraph office and wired a letter to Mark's family that he was safe and would contact them later by mail. He then planned to walk by the bank where his father used to work. On his way down Main Street he tried to stay under the extended eaves and porches to stay out of the worst of the rain. As he passed Doc Armstrong's office he looked into the window and saw Mary's parents inside. Adam looked pale with his arms around Jane who was sobbing and holding her head in her hands. Earl rushed inside. Both Adam and Jane looked up in complete surprise as if seeing a ghost. Both stood and rushed over to greet Earl. After the hugs and tears had abated Earl was told the story that John had died at sea during the storm. "Mary has run off and no one knows where she is. Earl, we fear the worst. She is pregnant with child and she has lost her beloved husband. She needs comforting and she needs someone around her who is rational. I fear she has already taken her own life. The sheriff and his men, the coast guard crew, and half the town are out looking for her. Earl, you are the only one who might know where she is hiding. Please, Earl, go find my Mary."

"Earl," Doc Armstrong said, "check with the Coast Guard station first before looking because they might have some better information as to where she has gone."

Earl rushed out the door and over to the Coast Guard Station. Jake was inside operating the radio.

" Anyone found Mary yet?" Earl said in a raised voice.

"Who are you?" Jake said.

"I'm a family friend," Earl said.

"This is all I know. When she found out John had drowned at sea she became distraught; and ran from our office crying. No one knows where she went. Everyone in town is out looking for her. My shift is over soon, and I'll be out searching too."

"Thanks," Earl said. He raced out the door, slamming it as he left. The rain still poured down and the wind was gusty. Earl ran towards the shoreline going through a small glade of firs and spruce. A large tree fell to the ground just ahead of him and he had to climb over its six-foot girth. On the other side and through the trees, he could see the waves crashing against the surf. He knew where Mary might be: the place they had gone to so many times as children. He at last came to the deer trail that wound up through the spruce forest and led to the cliff top that overlooked the Pacific.

Chapter 41

"What happened to Matt?" Luther demanded of River. They were in the speakeasy at the back of the Oriental building. The storm raged outside as Frank and River sat across from Luther.

"I heard he was gunned down on Main Street. He was trying to knife John Dowd, that basketball player," Frank said.

"This time John's made a big mistake," Luther said, slamming his shot glass against the wall as his face grew red and his brow furrowed.

"Stop the racket over there," shouted the bartender.

Luther picked up River's glass and threw it against the wall. He stood as the barkeep came rushing at him. Luther had his brass knuckles pulled tight over his fingers. He leveled the big bartender with a right punch to the head. Luther jumped on the downed man and smashed his fists into his face. He would have killed him had it not been for Frank and River pulling him off.

"Take your revenge on John Dowd, not the barkeep," River said, "Why not start with his beautiful wife. I heard she's pregnant."

"I'll kill them all," yelled Luther as he stalked out of the bar. He headed towards Mrs. Smith's boarding house.

With the brim of his hat shielding his eyes from the torrent of rain, Luther ran up the street towards the Smith residence. The hate dripped from his body as he remembered what drove him. He'd been put in prison unjustly, he'd been made to live like an animal in the forests, and his best friend had been gunned down. It was now time to get his revenge. Luther was like a wounded wild animal backed up against a wall and he wanted to rip the world to shreds. He looked through the kitchen window and saw Julia cooking at the stove. He remembered how Julia had shunned his advances and had made him feel small. It was now time for Julia to pay for her offense. It was time for everyone to pay. He went to the front and opened the squeaky screen door.

"Is that you, Jake?" Julia said. Before Julia had time to say another word Luther stood at the kitchen doorway. Behind him he heard Mrs. Smith's bedroom door open.

"Who's there?"

"It's me, Mrs. Smith, Luther Crabb."

Mrs. Smith yelled, "Get out of my house!" The front door opened with its squeak and Jake walked in. Luther grabbed Julia and pulled a knife from his belt. He held the knife's blade to Julia's throat. Jake and Mrs. Smith stood helpless at the kitchen door.

"Where's John Dowd?" Luther said.

"He died at sea this morning," Jake said.

"Oh no!" Julia said.

"Shut up," Luther said as he tightened his hold on Julia. "And his beautiful pregnant wife, where is she?"

"No one knows," Jake said.

There was a knock on the front door.

"That's just my neighbor, Bob," said Mrs. Smith. "He's bringing me a jug of moonshine."

"Go get the jug. One word about me being here, Julia's dead," Luther growled.

There was another knock on the door. Mrs. Smith

opened the front door.

"Here's your jug," Bob said. "It's fifty cents." Bob noticed Jake standing in the hall. "Hi, Jake," he said. Jake couldn't trust his mouth to return his greeting, and he didn't know what to do. His eyes were riveted on the knife and Luther.

"Say 'Hi' to the man," Luther whispered.

"Hi," Jake said.

"The money's in my bedroom, I'll get it for you," Mrs. Smith said.

"Hurry up," Luther whispered.

Mrs. Smith rushed back to the front door with the money. "Here you are, Bob." And then she shut the door. A few minutes later, Luther heard a footstep on the back porch and he turned his head to look. Jake lunged at Luther's arm with the knife and pulled it away, allowing Julia to spring free. Luther turned back and stuck the knife into Jake's midsection. Jake dropped to the floor. A bullet whizzed by Luther's head and he rushed out through the front door.

Another shot was fired as he fled down the street. He was running as fast as he could towards town. He stopped to get his breath beside a large cedar. The branches draped to the ground. He slithered under the cedar boughs and up against the trunk and rested, hidden from view. He peered out through the branches and up the street he could see the Smith house. Bob had gone back inside. Drops of water dribbled off the branches and down Luther's face. He had lost his hat while running.

Chapter 42

John roused himself; he was cold and wet as he lay on the beach. He was lucky he had not been crushed by the big chunks of driftwood next to him. The incoming tide had helped John swim to shore. Exhausted, he had fallen asleep as the tide went out. He shivered in the wet wind. His clothes were soaked. He remembered he had left some dry clothes at the boarding house. He groggily stood up and staggered towards town and Mrs. Smith's.

He knocked on the front door and Mrs. Smith answered. "John! We thought you were dead!"

"I would have been, but the currents helped me swim in. I did a stupid thing by diving for my watch and almost lost my life. I need my clothes and some rest," John said.

"Something bad just happened. Luther just stabbed Jake in the stomach. He would have killed Julia and me had it not been for my neighbor."

"Take me to Jake!"

Jake was on the kitchen floor. Julia was on her knees beside him, trying to cleanse the wound. Mrs. Smith told John that when she gave Bob his fifty cents she also gave him a scribbled note telling of their distress.

"Bob snuck around the house and scared Luther off with his gun, then went to get Dr. Armstrong."

"Luther left a few minutes ago. You must stop him," Jake said.

As he changed into dry clothes John said, "I've got to get him, before he kills someone else."

"Be careful; Luther has a knife and won't hesitate to use it," Julia said.

Jake whispered, "Mary thinks you are dead. She has run off and the whole town is looking for her. Don't worry about me, I'll be all right."

John didn't have time to rest. He ran out the front door and saw Bob and the doctor running up the street toward the boarding house. John thought as he ran past them, there's a madman loose and Mary thinks I'm dead. There's no telling what she is thinking at this moment. He knew he must find Mary first and then he would look for Luther. The first place he thought about looking was the cliffs overlooking the ocean, where the two of them had loved each other. He reached the sandy beach just as the tide was starting to come in. Huge waves crashed sending water that tugged at John's feet as he ran towards the path that led up to the cliff. The rain pounded down so thick he could barely make out the entrance through the forest.

Chapter 43

From his hiding place in the cedar, Luther watched as John went into the Smith home. Not long after, he saw John emerge and run right past where he hid. Luther came out of hiding and followed, staying a safe distance behind. Finally, Luther would have his opportunity; he had waited for this a long time. He followed John through the sand and surf to the cliff trail. John hadn't noticed him. Luther wiped the rain from his eyes and watched John ascend the trail. He vanished from sight in the heavy rain and dark forest shadows.

Chapter 44

Earl raced up the trail, but the wind was blowing so fiercely he could barely plod along. The ground was littered with broken branches and needles everywhere. He heard a loud crack as a tree snapped off at its midsection. A bolt of lightning struck and scorched another tree just ahead of him, and smoldered as he passed by. He climbed over logs and was scratched by debris. Small branches and twigs flew against his face and body. As he entered a clearing, a huge branch, known by loggers as a "widow-maker," crashed down from a spruce smacking his left leg near the knee. He felt the bone in his thigh snap, and fell to the ground.

He lay there in agony and realized he must get to the cliff top. He reached for a nearby branch, and broke it to the right size for a makeshift cane. He struggled to stand. The pain was too great, and he fell back to the ground. Pain was all he felt, then suddenly he saw John at his side.

"Are you real?" he asked, surprised to see him. John nodded.

"Thank God, you're alive! I heard you had died. I know Mary's up on the cliffs. You must get up there to help her," he went on.

"What's happened to you?" John asked.

"My leg is broken, I'll be okay, but I can't move. You must get to the cliff top, hurry!" John rushed up the trail.

A few minutes later Luther came into the clearing.

"Who are you?" Luther asked.

"I'm Earl, and a friend of Mary's."

"Did you see a man rush past you?" Luther asked.

"John just went up the trail. He might need your help, so hurry!" He watched Luther pick up a big branch. "What are you doing?" Earl said.

"Why, I'm going to kill you," he said in a sinister voice. "I plan to kill them, too," he added, nodding toward the top of the cliff.

"I haven't done anything to hurt you!

"Your death will be quick," Luther said. Earl tried to defend himself with his cane, but he had little energy left. Luther smashed the large branch into Earl's face, and his world went black.

Chapter 45

John ran up the steep rocky trail as it zigzagged towards the summit. His breath almost gone, he neared the top of the bluff. Slowly he climbed over the edge and, to his great relief, he saw Mary sitting on a rock, her attention focused out to sea. Her wavy hair hung limp and straight on her head, her clothes were drenched, and every once in a while she would flail her fist and scream at the sea. John could hear the waves as they crashed against the rocks far below.

Over the thundering surf, the howling wind and the driving rain, John heard Mary's voice as she spoke to God and the sea. "What kind of God are you? Why do you take a good man's life? He was a saint! He was an honorable man, the world needs people like John, why did you take him?"

Then she stood and slowly walked towards the edge of the cliff. As she reached the edge, John called out to her, "Mary, wait, it's me! John!" She turned and there in front of her was John. He saw that she was stunned, thinking he must be a ghost. The wind blew with such force that Mary was nearly blown off the cliff. Rain beat down on her and onto the ground forming rivulets that ran under her feet and dripped off the edge into the sea below. If Mary took one step back she would be gone forever. John fell to his knees.

"Mary, you must believe me, I am your husband. I've come here a new man. I'm here as your lover and husband. I love you, do you understand me? I love you, a genuine love more powerful than the mighty storm that's blowing. I'm no longer tethered to that watch, I no longer fear the future. I understand now how much you love me. Come here and let me hold you. Please, Mary, please come here."

John watched the confusion on her face. He feared she would step back and he would lose her forever. And if he stepped toward her, he knew she might take that backward step. She finally saw him, and as her eyes widened, she ran towards John.

"John, Luther's behind you!" Mary screamed. John jumped up, quickly turned around. Not far off stood a gloating Luther Crabb. In his right hand he held a knife and on his fingers were the brass knuckles. Mary reached John and clung to him. Luther stalked a little closer; John could see the madness in his eyes.

"Go away and leave us alone!" Mary said.

He was five feet from them and closing in. John instinctively felt for his watch. It was gone. He was about to push Mary aside and rush at Luther, but Mary was holding him so tightly he couldn't move her away. He thought of picking her up and retreating backwards, but behind them was a sheer cliff with the ocean and rocks fifty feet below. There was nowhere to go. Luther laughed. His big knife gleamed as he held it above his head. He roared above the downpour and the thunder, "Matt, it's our time for revenge!"

A sudden bolt of lightning silhouetted Luther against the dark sky. He charged at them like a wild bull...and then stopped in mid-charge as they heard a thump. Luther's chest arched outward and his swing with the knife went wild, missing both Mary and John. Luther fell to the ground writhing in pain. There was a knife in his back.

Behind Luther and barely visible in the downpour

was Earl lying on the ground. The couple rushed over to him. John gently turned him on his side. He was breathing in heavy rasping gasps. John could see he didn't have long to live.

"Oh, Earl," Mary said, as she gently put her arms around him and held him close. She kissed his lips.

"My beautiful Mary, please forgive me for what I did."

"Yes, of course I forgive you," Mary replied.

"I want to tell John something," Earl said in a barely audible voice. Mary moved aside and motioned to John. John put his ear close to Earl's mouth.

"Promise me you will take care of her," Earl whispered, gasping for breath.

"I swear. I will cherish and love her with all my heart until the day I die," John whispered.

Earl's eyes turned to look at John, and instead of hatred for a rival suitor, John saw respect and love. He breathed his last breath shortly after John's promise.

Mary couldn't stop crying. She clung to Earl's body and rocked him as John stood above them.

The rain clouds began dispersing. A few patches of blue sky broke free. A ray of sunlight highlighted their position on the cliff.

Robert came into view as he and four men were running up the path. When they reached the top, Robert embraced John and Mary. Mary was still crying, and John explained to Robert what had taken place.

"Is Jake all right?" John asked.

"Yes, he'll be fine," Robert said. "He's the one who told us to come up here."

Robert ordered his men to take the bodies to the morgue. The three friends descended from the cliff, heading back towards town.

"I thought you were drowned for sure," Robert

said. "When you dove off the boat a big wave pushed us away from the spot where you entered the water. We thought we had motored back to that spot but were unable to see you. We stayed there for two hours before I decided to return to port."

"I dove after my watch," John said. "Ted dropped it into the sea. It's funny; I really thought that watch was my lucky piece, that it was responsible for the good things that happened to me. Had I continued swimming after it I would have drowned. I always believed it was that watch that gave me Mary, and you and Jake as my friends. I didn't have the inner strength to believe in myself. When I saw that watch disappear, at first I felt helpless, that I would surely drown. Then a new strength energized me; I realized I was at last on my own. It was as if I had suddenly grown wings and flew away from my reliance on that heirloom."

He put his arm around Mary. "I now know that Mary loves me for me and I no longer harbor jealous thoughts about her. She is the greatest gift I could ever receive."

"That being said, I think Ted threw your watch into the ocean on purpose," Robert said. "He meant for you to drown. It was no accident as he claims. I will do my best to have him drummed out of the Coast Guard. He's the last of Evans' henchman and I will be glad when he is gone."

Epilogue

It was a while before life returned to normal around Bandon. The population was busy cleaning up after the destructive storm. The days that followed were clear and sunny with beautiful evening sunsets. The tragic shipwrecks were now in the past. Investigations determined that the shipwrecks resulted from the weather, acts of God. Robert succeeded in having Ted Burns drummed out of the Coast Guard. Burns left town and was never heard from again.

Then, there was Earl's funeral to arrange. At the ceremony, he was highly praised for saving John and Mary from certain death. Earl had been a true hero. His remains were buried in the Bandon Cemetery that overlooks the bay and the Pacific Ocean.

Not long after that, Mary gave birth to a boy, who had a happy disposition, and thick curly black hair. His parents named him John, Junior. Later, they had two more childen.

John, along with his two buddies, remained in the United States Coast Guard. Robert Crowe became a District Superintendent. Jake recovered from his knife wound and he and Julia had four children.

Doug Gilbertson inherited his father's lumber company. He married Lucy and was a leading member of the Coos Bay Community. Earl's cousin Mark married Belinda and worked at Doug's lumber mill. Doug made arrangements for Mark to attend an accounting school so he could take care of the mill's books.

The Nestlé building never housed another food manufacturing business. During World War II it housed United States Army vehicles and equipment. Eventually, it was bought by a large lumber company. In 2001 it was razed.

On his eighteen birthday John Dowd Jr. was presented with a special gift from his father. The package was wrapped in bright red paper, and when John Jr. unwrapped it, he found to his delight a mahogany-framed parchment, about eight inches by ten inches, to be used as a wall hanging. Written on the parchment in special calligraphy were the words: "In the confusion of life persevere."

About the Author

Joe Blakely has spent most of his life in Oregon. After careers in real estate, furniture repair and refinishing, and the University of Oregon Office of Public Safety, he retired in 1999 and began pursuing his love of photography and history.

Joe is the author of two previous books, *The Tall Firs: The Story of the University of Oregon and The First NCAA Basketball Championship*, published in 2004. This book was exhibited by The North American Society for Sport History. His other book is *The Bellfountain Giant Killers, the Story of a Small Oregon High School and its Miraculous Championship Season* of 1937, published in 2003. He has also written a screen play about the Bellfountain Giant Killers which is registered with the Writer's Guild of America.

Photo by Saundra Miles

In 2003, the *Oregon Historical Quarterly* published his article "The Nestlé Condensary in Bandon." Visits to conduct research at the Bandon Historical Society Museum gave him access to photographs of the small Oregon coast town and led to his discovery of a photograph that started him wondering about who the people in the photos were and what their lives might have been like.

This book is an effort to put names and faces to the tumultuous events surrounding the Nestlé Condensary's time in Bandon, the townspeople's struggles to find a decent living, the always-present danger of sea and storm, and the good and bad people who made Bandon their home.

Blakely　　　　　　The Heirloom

Order Form

Autographed copies of this or Joe Blakely's other two books may be ordered from the author.

COPIES   TITLE   PRICE   TOTAL

_____   The Heirloom $15.00   _____

_____   The Tall Firs: The Story of the $9.95   _____
                 University of Oregon and The First NCAA Basketball Championship

_____   The Bellfountain Giant Killers, $9.95   _____
                 the Story of a Small Oregon High School and its Miraculous Championship Season

Please include $2.50 shipping and handling for one book, and $1.50 for each additional book. Payment must accompany orders. Allow 3 weeks for delivery.

My check or money order is enclosed for $_____ .

Name _____

Organization _____

Address _____

City/State/Zip _____

Phone _____ Email _____

Make check payable to:

Joe R. Blakely

P.O. Box 40113

Eugene Oregon 97404

Order Form

Autographed copies of this or Joe Blakely's other two books may be ordered from the author.

COPIES	TITLE	PRICE	TOTAL
_____	The Heirloom	$15.00	_____
_____	The Tall Firs: The Story of the University of Oregon and The First NCAA Basketball Championship	$9.95	_____
_____	The Bellfountain Giant Killers, the Story of a Small Oregon High School and its Miraculous Championship Season	$9.95	_____

Please include $2.50 shipping and handling for one book, and $1.50 for each additional book. Payment must accompany orders. Allow 3 weeks for delivery.

My check or money order is enclosed for $_____ .

Name _____

Organization _____

Address _____

City/State/Zip _____

Phone _____ Email _____

Make check payable to:

Joe R. Blakely

P.O. Box 40113

Eugene Oregon 97404